One of the Boys

Heartlines

Books by Pam Lyons

A Boy Called Simon
He Was Bad
It Could Never Be
Latchkey Girl
Danny's Girl
Odd Girl Out
Ms Perfect

Books by Anita Eires

Tug Of Love
Summer Awakening
Spanish Exchange
Star Dreamer
Californian Summer
If Only . . .
Teacher's Pet
Working Girl

Books by Mary Hooper

Love Emma XXX
Follow That Dream
My Cousin Angie
Happy Ever After
Opposites Attract
A Love Like Yours

Books by Barbara Jacobs

Two Times Two

Books by Jane Pitt

Loretta Rose
Autumn Always Comes
Stony Limits
Rainbows For Sale
Pia
The Boy Who Was Magic

Books by Ann de Gale

Island Encounter
Hands Off

Books by Anthea Cohen

Dangerous Love

Books by David S Williams

Give Me Back My Pride
Forgive and Forget
My Life to Live

Books by Jill Young

Change of Heart
Three Summers On

Books by Ann Ruffell

Friends For Keeps
Secret Passion
Baby Face

Books by Lorna Read

Images
The Name Is Zero

Books by Jane Butterworth

Spotlight On Sam

Books by John Harvey

Wild Love
Last Summer, First Love

Books by Anita Davies

Stepsisters

Heartlines

♥

Pam Lyons

One of the Boys

For Gerry, the mechanic
in my life.

A Pan Original

First published 1987 by Pan Books Ltd,
Cavaye Place, London SW10 9PG
9 8 7 6 5 4 3 2 1
© Pam Lyons 1987
ISBN 0 330 29885 2

Printed and bound in Great Britain by
Richard Clay Ltd, Bungay, Suffolk

This book is sold subject to the condition that it
shall not, by way of trade or otherwise, be lent, re-sold,
hired out or otherwise circulated without the publisher's prior
consent in any form of binding or cover other than that in which
it is published and without a similar condition including this
condition being imposed on the subsequent purchaser.

Chapter 1

'Gerry, just look at your nails!'

Engrossed in conversation with her brother Bobby about the intricacies of fitting a new exhaust pipe, Gerry didn't hear her mother's complaint until it was repeated.

'What about them?' she asked, perplexed, then smiled as she noticed the reason for her mother's comment. 'It's HMP,' she explained, as if that pardoned her for coming to the lunch table with nails in mourning.

Mary Jones let out a sigh. 'I know what it is, Gerry,' she said, half-resignedly. 'I haven't been married to the owner of Jones' Garage and Services for the past twenty-odd years without becoming an expert in different lubricants. What I'm trying to say, pet, is that you should scrub up before sitting down.'

Gerry pulled a wry face. 'You never go on at the men about their hands,' she said.

'It's part of their jobs, Gerry. It's not yours.' Her mother informed her pleasantly but firmly.

'Yet,' Gerry put in.

'We'll see about that,' her mother replied. Then added, 'When you've finished your meal, love, you can give me a hand with the puddings.'

Gerry nodded, as she stared absent-mindedly at the portion of shepherd's pie still left on her plate. A second later, her large blue eyes were back on her brother; soon she was again deeply engrossed with the details of the exhaust. The remains of her lunch, as well as her mother's request for help were forgotten.

'Gerry! Are you going to give me a hand?' Her mother's voice had a slight edge to it.

'Coming!' she called through to the kitchen; then, as she glanced up, she caught her father's eye. 'I was just going, Dad,' she said, a spark of red appearing on her freckled cheeks. 'Anyway, I don't see why it always has to be *me* who helps out round the kitchen,' she added half to herself, as she gathered the dirty plates off the table.

'It's a woman's work!' said Jeremy, her eldest brother, a glint of mischief in his hazel eyes.

'Good training for when you're older,' added Mike, one of the mechanics, jokingly.

'The trouble with you lot is that you've never heard of equality – or Women's Lib!' she said haughtily, nose in the air as she made her way through to the kitchen with the pile of dirty plates.

'What was that, dear?' her mother asked as Gerry placed the dishes on the worktop. Mrs Jones was in the process of pouring a pan of piping-hot custard into a pottery jug. Several portions of apple pie sat waiting on the counter.

'Women's Lib, that's what! Life's different today. Men and women are equal – there's not one set of rules for one lot, and a different set for the others.'

'Oh? Well, that's as may be, dear,' her mother answered, 'but equality won't get an apple pie baked on Saturdays – nor will it stop that same apple pie from getting cold if it isn't taken through to be eaten this minute. Now, off you go!' She turned Gerry round to face the door and gave her a little push to help her on her way, then followed her out of the kitchen.

'All right then, boys?' Mrs Jones asked, as the pudding rapidly vanished to exclamations of appreciation.

'Is there any more, Mum?' asked Sam, the youngest Jones boy, minutes later, finishing his pie with a lick of his lips.

Sam was a year older than Gerry but they looked like twins. He had the same springy, copper-coloured hair, the same unusual dark-blue eyes, and the same tall, lithe figure.

'There's a couple more portions,' Mary Jones told her son, reaching across to take his empty plate, but Sam stopped her and stood up.

'It's okay, Mum, I'll get it myself,' he said, then let his gaze run round the table. 'Anyone else for more?' His eyes rested on Mike, who refused, then on to his brothers Jeremy and Bobby, and finally on his father. Only Jeremy and Bobby confessed to having room in their stomachs for more. Sam took his brothers' proffered plates. 'See, little sis,' he said as he passed Gerry's chair, 'we men don't mind helping.'

'Let's see if you're still so helpful when it comes to clearing the table and washing up!' Gerry called, after Sam's retreating back. It was said casually, but there was a definite sharpness underlining her words.

'Gerry!' She turned her attention back to her mother and saw the warning look in those clear grey eyes.

'Well . . .' Gerry began, then stopped. There was no need to get herself in a temper over the injustice of it all, she thought, chewing on her bottom lip again. Life, she decided for the umpteenth time, would have been far simpler if she had not broken the Jones trend by being born a girl rather than a boy.

As it was, for sixteen years it had been an uphill struggle to prove herself equal to, if not better than, her three brothers. And it didn't help that her mother seemed set on turning her into a Barbie Doll. Although, Gerry mused, to be more honest she was more like a Cabbage Patch Doll, what with her turned-up nose and mass of unruly red hair.

'You sulking?' her father now asked, from across the table.

Gerry snapped back into the present. 'Me? Don't be silly! Sulking? Of course not!'

Her father, lighting his pipe, peered at her through the billowing blue smoke then, taking the pipe from his lips, he examined the tobacco before returning his gaze to rest on her. 'Oh?' was all he said. Then he grinned.

'What are you laughing at?' Gerry asked, feeling slightly riled.

Mr Jones took his pipe from his mouth, reached across, and squeezed her hand gently. 'Don't get your knickers in a twist,' he told her, kindly. 'I was just thinking how difficult it must be for you, the only girl growing up in a houseful of men, that's all.'

Gerry stood up and looked at the sea of smiling faces round the table. 'It's only difficult because you all insist on differentiating between the sexes,' she proclaimed loftily. 'It's not difficult . . . not for me. I'm quite happy just being a person. I really don't see that there's any need for the fact that you're men, and I'm a girl, to come into it. After all, as far as I'm concerned there's no difference between men and women.'

She let out a somewhat theatrical sigh, then turned

to join her mother in the kitchen, followed by loud shouts of 'Get her!' and 'Who are you kidding, little sis?' Then a round of applause filled the air.

'Forget it, pet,' Mrs Jones advised her daughter. As she passed Gerry to get more dirty dishes to stack into the dishwasher, she stopped and gave her a quick hug.

For a moment, Gerry hugged her mother back, then pulled away. After all, it didn't do to look soft, did it? Not when you were surrounded by a houseful of men.

'Why don't you go and get on with whatever you were doing before lunch, pet?' her mother now suggested, helpfully.

'But don't you want a hand?' Gerry asked, beginning to feel a bit guilty for not offering in the first place.

'The dishwasher does it all, really. And besides, it's such a nice day, it's a shame not to make the most of it. Why don't you give your friend Patsie a ring and arrange to go out for the afternoon?'

Gerry shook her head. 'Patsie's probably spending the day with Clive Rowlings.'

'Clive Rowlings,' Gerry's mother repeated. 'I guess he's Patsie's latest boyfriend, then?'

Gerry nodded and remarked, 'But Clive seems all right – much nicer than the blokes Patsie normally goes out with.' She went on, 'Well, if you're sure you don't need me, I'd like to get on with dismantling the exhaust from that latest MG chassis Mike found for me. It looks really sound.'

Mary Jones nearly laughed out loud at her daughter's mounting excitement.

Gerry eyed her mother in exasperation. 'So now what's funny?' she asked.

'Nothing, pet,' her mother tried to assure her. 'It's

just that most girls get excited about new clothes, or a special boy, but not my daughter. Oh no! What does she get excited about? Building a sports car!'

'Rebuilding,' Gerry corrected, then grinned. 'But, Mum, what a classic car! Have you ever seen a real MG J2, 1934 model? What a vintage!' Her eyes began to sparkle with sapphire lights. 'They were some cars. Beautiful!'

'Okay – okay. I've got the message, sweet. So you're in love with a dream – that's fine. So off you go and cuddle up to your exhaust.' Her mother said it banteringly, and Gerry took it in good spirits.

'The trouble is, Mum,' Gerry threw over her shoulder as she let herself out of the back door, 'you really don't understand.'

Chapter 2

Whistling the latest Paul King single, Gerry stepped out on to the sunlit forecourt. She was now dressed, as usual, in her tan overalls, her mop of red curls pushed out of sight under her cap with a few tendrils escaping to frame her face.

'If you need any help with dismantling that exhaust, give me a call. I'll be in the service bay,' Mike yelled across to her.

'Okay. Thanks!' Gerry called back.

The way she said it got a quick wink from Mike, who added, with his lopsided grin, 'Though knowing you, you probably won't need any help, will you?'

'Probably not,' Gerry breezed. 'Still, don't be upset, it's nice to know the offer's there.' She went back to her whistling as she headed round the side of the forecourt to the back of the garage, to what the family referred to as the Big Tin Barn — a vast, hangar-type building which was used for storing spare parts as well as acting as a second workshop area.

Five minutes later, all that could be seen of Gerry was a pair of feet in black rubber boots protruding from under an old, jacked-up chassis. The whistling was soon replaced by a gentle tapping as she manoeuvred her spanner round the rusted bolts which held the exhaust on to its old manifold.

'You all right under there, kid?' Her brother Bobby's voice filtered through to her, some time later. 'Just kick your heels if the answer's "yes".'

Gerry kicked her heels on the asphalt.

'Okay,' he called back. 'I'm going into the house to brew up some tea. I'll bring you a mug out, right?'

Again the small pair of booted feet beat a tattoo on the ground. At the other end, Gerry had just felt the first grating movement of the bolt turning under the pressure of the spanner. She gave a whoop of delight — and was rewarded with a mouthful of rust chippings!

When Bobby returned five minutes later, he burst out laughing. Gerry's face was pitch black under the safety goggles!

'Uh, sis, if you're trying to impress some bloke,' Bobby remarked with a grin, 'I think you put too much make up on.'

'That's not funny!' Gerry warned, glaring up at him with her dark-blue eyes blazing through the sooty layer covering her face.

Bobby crouched beside her, a mug of tea in each hand. 'Here,' – he offered her the nearest one – 'swill your mouth out with some of this.'

Obediently, Gerry removed her goggles and seized the mug. A second later, her good humour returned.

'I suppose I forgot,' she admitted, between mouthfuls of the hot brew. 'Never open your mouth under a car, eh?' She swallowed the last of the tea.

Gerry handed Bobby the enamel mug and was about to head back under the car when she saw her brother stop in his tracks.

'Hey, kid!' he called across to her. She looked at him and pulled a silly face. Bobby laughed and retraced his steps. 'Listen – I forgot to tell you. Mum said your sidekick, Patsie, rang – you're to ring her back before six.'

'What for?' Gerry was slightly irritated that she'd have to break off from unscrewing the bolts – especially as now one of them had actually budged.

Bobby shrugged. 'Search me, kid,' he replied. 'Mum didn't say.' He turned to go but Gerry caught his arm and, hitching up his sleeve, craned her neck to look at his watch.

'Oh, I've got hours yet,' she said.

Bobby reclaimed his arm. 'Hours for what?'

'Unscrewing the bolt that's just shifted before ringing Patsie, of course, thicko.'

Bobby grinned. 'Of course. How stupid of me. Priorities first.'

'Of course! Whatever Patsie wants will probably wait – unless she wants to borrow some of my clothes for her date with Clive Rowlings,' she added. 'That's probably why she wants me to ring her before six, come to think of it.'

'You girls make me laugh,' Bobby remarked, raising his eyebrows and shaking his head. 'The things you get up to to impress us blokes.' He laughed and turned away, but not before Gerry had retorted with, 'Some girls may – I don't! Got it?'

'You're right, kid!' her brother threw back over his retreating shoulder. 'You're not a normal type of girl, are you? We all know you're unique.'

It was said in a light-hearted, bantering tone but somehow, as Gerry wriggled her slim body back under the old MG, she wasn't quite sure if she liked the implication. Just because she preferred tinkering around with old cars to making awkward conversation with a dull date, and read car magazines instead of romance stories, didn't mean she was any less feminine than Patsie – or any of her other girlfriends, come to that!

With renewed vigour she went back to wrestling with the bolt, easing it round until she felt it giving a bit more. For a second she visualized her friend. Sure, Patsie was pretty, especially with her long black hair pulled back from her face so that the full length of it fell straight down her back like a thick ribbon of rippling blue-black silk. Patsie also liked to wear pretty, feminine clothes and experimented with her mother's eye make-up, but so what? When they were both in their regulation school skirts and blouses, Gerry mused, they both looked equally feminine, didn't they?

Men! Gerry thought, angrily. Why did they always have to slot every girl into a neat little pigeonhole? Look at what happened at school when she'd informed the headmaster that she was more interested in taking

Metalwork classes than Home Economics!

'But . . . well, it's very unusual,' Mr Carpenter had stammered, peering at Gerry with owl-like curiosity across his steel-rimmed spectacles. 'Very – unusual . . .'

Gerry hadn't said anything – mainly because she couldn't see what was so unusual about wanting to learn metalwork. Her brothers all had and it had been invaluable when they'd all opted to follow in their father's business.

'Do your parents know about this?' Mr Carpenter inquired, as though Gerry had asked to be allowed to indulge in a subject that somehow wasn't appropriate for a girl.

'Yes,' she informed the head.

'And?' The owl-like eyes zoned in on her.

Gerry shrugged and nervously ran her fingers through her hair, sending it, as usual, into a wide, springy halo. 'They said it was up to me,' she said.

'I see.' Mr Carpenter's reply had come with such a whoosh that Gerry felt certain he didn't 'see' at all. And certainly, he wasn't pleased about the request.

'Many schools have mixed classes now,' Gerry continued, but the frozen look on Mr Carpenter's face suddenly made her wish she had kept her mouth closed. Mr Carpenter obviously wasn't pleased that Gerry considered his school behind the times.

'Yes. Well, we'll have to see about this – er – special request.' From the way this last sentence was delivered, Gerry had gathered the conversation was at an end. As she turned to leave the head's study, Mr Carpenter asked, 'Would you be very upset if you weren't able to take the subject, Geraldine?'

Gerry felt it was said in such a way, and in such a tone that he expected her to say no, she didn't really mind. But the truth was that she did mind and she had told him so, in what she hoped was a firm and confident voice, then quickly left the room.

Now Gerry laid the spanner on the ground beside her and began to unscrew the rest of the bolt with her fingers. She couldn't really see what all the fuss was about. Why, women were employed in *all* areas of industry now, weren't they? So why all the hullabaloo just because she preferred to know how to weld two pieces of metal, rather than make flaky pastry?

The bolt twisted down to the last thread – then stuck. 'Damn!' Gerry hissed through gritted teeth. She reached for the spanner to force the bolt free.

It wouldn't move – not even a fraction.

Gerry closed her eyes, then tightened her grip on the spanner with both hands and tried again. It has to give, she told herself. Again the spanner grated against the rusted metal, without moving the bolt. With aching arms, Gerry decided to give it one last try.

If you move this time, she vowed to herself, I'll give it a rest for today and go and ring Patsie. She concentrated on her final effort. She expected to have to really push hard – but miraculously, this time, just the slightest movement with the spanner and the nut passed over the last thread and fell, with a thud, on to the ground beside her.

For a second, Gerry couldn't believe her luck. She put the spanner back on the ground and felt round for the offending bolt. It didn't take long to locate the thick, rusted piece of metal. Without thinking, she raised her head to look at it – and immediately wished she hadn't as the warm flesh of her forehead collided with the cold hard steel of the car.

'Oo-ww!' Her cry of pain echoed in her ringing ears. For a moment she lay still, shocked by the sudden impact. Then, as quickly as she could, she slid her slender body out from underneath the car and sat cross-legged on the ground. With tentative fingers Gerry examined the rising egg-shaped bump. She thought she must look like a remake of Lady Frankenstein!

'Hey, Gerry!' It was Mike, strolling round from the service bay area. When he saw Gerry sitting on the ground with a pained expression on her face, he began to run. 'What happened?' he called, his voice full of concern.

Gerry waved her free hand in reassurance that everything was all right. But he came over to her, just the same.

'Let me look.' He lifted her to her feet with one swift, easy movement.

'It's nothing, Mike,' Gerry insisted. 'I just made the classic mistake of sitting up under a car, that's all.'

'That's enough, isn't it?' His voice was solicitous, his fingers gentle as they removed hers to let him examine the damage. 'Wow! Nice one, kid!' He let out a short sigh. 'You're so unhappy with the head you've got, you've got to grow another, is that it?'

Gerry laughed – even though she was aware of a throbbing pain mounting at her temple. 'Does it show much?' she asked, after a second.

Mike looked at her forehead, then into her worried

eyes. 'What do you want me to say? Of course it shows! Now come on, let's get you into the house and put some ice on that before it takes off.'

It was half-past five by the time Gerry had bathed, washed her hair, changed into clean jeans and sweatshirt, then decided she'd better ring Patsie.

She took the phone into her bedroom and sat at the top of her bed, curling her long legs under her and resting her back against the wall. Then she dialled the number.

'What kept you, Gerry?' asked her best friend, a peeved tone underlying her voice.

'I – er – I'm sorry. I got caught up,' Gerry said, feeling slightly guilty, yet niggled at the same time. Patsie always seemed to expect her to be on call every second of the day.

'What with?' Patsie now asked, adding, 'No! Don't tell me! Let me guess. Was it a new fan belt? Or perhaps you had a date with a set of sparking plugs?'

'Okay – when you've finished, what was it you wanted?' Gerry was used to her friend's barbs – and most times she laughed them off. Only sometimes, like now when her head was still aching, she wasn't in a laughing mood.

'You don't have to sound like that.' Patsie's voice took on a more gentle tone. 'Only I did ring you two hours ago . . .' she reminded her.

'One hour,' Gerry corrected, wearily. Patsie always did exaggerate.

'Right – but your mum said you were only round the back, so what took you so long?'

'Let's say I had a struggle on my hands,' Gerry said,

softening a little at her friend's peeved tone.

'Not with the hunky Mike, was it?'

Gerry let out a sigh and told Patsie about the bump she'd received while working on her car. 'Besides, Mike's married, remember?' she said, her fingers carefully examining the circumference of the newly acquired extension on her forehead.

'People get divorced,' Patsie put in.

'People who are unhappy, maybe. Mike's very happily married and besides, he's twenty-four.'

'Older men are far more interesting.' Patsie let out a deep sigh.

Suddenly, Gerry's fingers found the tender part of the bump. She winced. 'Come on, Patsie,' she said, 'you didn't want me to ring you to have a chat about Mike, did you?'

'No – well, actually, you're right. It's about tonight.'

Gerry shifted her weight off her ankles and straightened her long legs. 'What about tonight?'

'You doing anything?' Patsie asked.

Gerry instantly became suspicious. 'Why?'

'Stop being so sceptical for heaven's sake,' her friend countered. 'Are you free? Yes – or no?'

Gerry hedged. 'Depends . . .' she said.

'That means yes. Good! We'll pick you up around seven-thirty. Wear something pretty and for goodness' sake, do something with your hair – okay?'

'No!' Gerry almost shouted down the line.

'What do you mean, no? Haven't I got your best interests at heart, Gerry? Don't I always try and do things to please you?'

That was true. Gerry couldn't deny her friend's great big heart. It was just that Patsie's idea of doing Gerry a good turn didn't always coincide with Gerry's own idea of what was good for her.

Gerry's silence proved to be all the licence Patsie needed. 'See you later, Gerry-baby!' she breezed down the line.

'But – just a sec – ' The line went dead.

For a minute Gerry sat on the bed and stared at the phone, then decided to ring back and tell Patsie to count her out of whatever it was she'd lined up for the evening.

When she'd dialled the last digit, the engaged signal came over the line. Angry, she replaced the receiver and waited a few minutes before trying again. But when she redialled, it was still engaged. Either Patsie was ringing every one of her friends, or she'd taken the phone off the hook. Maybe while she had a bath – or to stop me ringing back to cancel, Gerry thought. She wouldn't put anything past Patsie.

As it was, she was a bit tired of the way Patsie was forever trying to think up ploys to get her to be what Patsie termed 'more sociable'. Why she still bothered, Gerry didn't know. After the number of times she'd let Patsie down by not going along with her prearranged foursomes, or blind dates, anyone else would have given Gerry up as a dead loss!

But that was Patsie – always trying. The trouble was, as Gerry had tried to explain time and again, most of the boys Patsie thought would interest her best friend just weren't her type at all. They only seemed to be interested in football, the latest rave group, or their own images. If they were interested in cars at all, it either extended only as far as the back seat, or they couldn't believe a mere female knew so much about vintage models, or the workings of engines. Gerry was fed up with Patsie's attempts at matchmaking.

She glanced at the clock and discovered it was nearly seven. She tried Patsie's number once more, then gave up. This time no answer, which meant her best friend was probably already on her way.

A sigh of exasperation escaped Gerry's lips. There was no alternative but to get herself ready – but for what?

Walking over to the dressing-table mirror, she leaned forward to examine her face. Le Bump was really rather amazing, rising as it did like a miniature Mount Etna out of her pale forehead. She toyed for a moment with the idea of brushing her hair forward to try to cover it, then dismissed the notion as silly. If she did that, her hair would have to cover her entire face!

Extra eye make-up might take the attention away from it, Gerry thought, remembering an article she'd once read in one of Patsie's fashion magazines about emphasizing your good points and taking attention away from your bad ones. She certainly wasn't a make-up expert, but she'd have a go . . .

By the time she'd finished applying several shades of her mother's lavender and blue eye-shadow, as well as three layers of mascara, Gerry decided she looked like someone with a severe case of insomnia! She had managed to disguise the pale, egg-shaped lump so that it blended better with the rest of her face, but she could still see a faint outline.

So what, I don't care anyway! she convinced herself as she took a final appraisal in the mirror. She'd at least made an effort by changing out of her jeans and sweatshirt. She now wore her best all-in-one grey jumpsuit in satinized quilted cotton, teamed with her favourite sapphire-coloured teeshirt. Actually, she decided, with her mixture of red hair and pale skin, the colours looked great.

Shame about the bump, though, she thought. Then giggled. It could always serve as a talking point if the company proved dull. And at least her headache had gone.

Chapter 3

'Patsie's calling round any second, Mum,' Gerry said, jumping the last two stairs. She landed with a light thud beside her mother, who was busy arranging fresh daffodils and tulips in a vase on the hall table. Flower arranging was the latest subject Mary Jones was taking at evening classes at the local Institute.

'There, aren't they lovely?' Asked her mother.

'Very nice,' Gerry said, trying to muster enthusiasm. Flowers were flowers, after all. 'It's okay if I go out this evening, then?' Her mother was playing with a pink tulip which apparently had a will of its own.

'I should think so, as long as you're not home too late.' Mrs Jones propped the errant tulip behind one of the taller daffodils, then turned to her daughter and gave her a delighted smile.

'Now, you actually look like my daughter!' she said, slipping a hand under Gerry's hair and lifting it free of her collar. 'I just wish you'd wear a skirt sometimes, pet. I'm sure most people don't believe you've actually got a fine pair of legs; no one ever sees them.'

'Leave off, Mum, do!' Gerry said, sidestepping another attempt to fluff out her hair.

'It's not right that a pretty girl like you shouldn't make the most of her looks.' Her mother ran an approving eye over her daughter's trim appearance. 'But I must say, this evening you look lovely! Now,' she busied herself with again rearranging the flowers, as the wayward tulip had decided to leave the daffodil's embrace, 'where are you off to?'

'I don't know. Patsie didn't actually say. But I won't be late,' Gerry added. She was quite prepared to leave Patsie's arranged outing if she was bored. It wouldn't be the first time she had left early, or was bored, she thought.

'I thought you said Patsie was dating that nice Clive Rowlings?'

It often amazed Gerry just what her mother remembered. 'She is – I think.' She nodded at her mother through the hall mirror as she stole another glance at her forehead. Le Bump still hadn't done a disappearing trick – yet – even though she had managed to conceal it quite well.

'Does that mean you're tagging along – or has she got another blind date lined up for you, love?' Her mother decided to let the tulip find its own way in the world, and walked towards the sitting-room.

'I told you, Mum,' Gerry called after her, a thin note of exasperation touching her tone, 'she didn't say anything – only that she'd be here about now.'

As if on cue, there was a loud honking of a car horn from the forecourt.

Gerry pulled the net curtain aside from the glass panelling on the front door and saw Patsie piling out of Clive's father's bright red hatchback.

As she opened the door, the hooter sounded again.

'Come on, we'll be late!' Patsie called across to her. Gerry took in the total effect of her friend's clinging cream stretch satin trousers and T-shirt, topped with a huge, floppy cerise cardigan and matching ankle boots, and suddenly felt frumpy and old-fashioned.

'Have a good time, pet!' her mother called, as Gerry grabbed her shoulder bag, then headed for the car.

'Hi, Mrs Jones!' Patsie called across the expanse of forecourt and garden to where Gerry's mother stood in the open doorway. 'Everything okay?'

'Yes, thank you, Patsie dear,' came the reply over Gerry's head. Then her mother added, 'You look very stunning, if I may say so.'

Patsie's cheeks flushed with pleasure, and she smiled happily. 'What, in this old thing?' she teased.

As Patsie stepped round the car to greet Gerry, a chorus of wolf whistles echoed across from the service bay. Patsie and Gerry turned to see Gerry's three brothers and Mike ogling them.

Patsie, delighted with all the attention, made a great show of throwing them all kisses – which immediately met with more shouts of appreciation.

Gerry grabbed Patsie's arm and pulled her towards the car, where a frozen-faced Clive Rowlings sat tapping out a tattoo on his father's steering wheel.

'When the show's over we'll get on our way, shall we, girls?' he said. Then he greeted Gerry with a warm smile. 'Hi!'

Gerry smiled back and clambered into the rear seat, while Patsie manoeuvred herself carefully into the front.

'That's the trouble with these ski pants,' she moaned, when she'd finally got herself comfortable. 'It's okay when you're standing – but a bit of a problem when it comes to knee-bends.'

'You sure you shouldn't have got a size larger?' Clive asked, throwing a wink over his shoulder to Gerry. As he started the engine and put the car into reverse, she ducked so that Clive could get a better view.

'They're not tight!' Patsie asserted, tartly.

'No. Of course they're not,' Clive agreed without conviction.

Taking offence, Patsie tossed her long ponytail back off her shoulder – and nearly hit Gerry's face with it.

'Hey! Watch it, Patsie, will you!' Gerry moved to one side and stared through the window as Clive edged the car out into the Saturday-night traffic.

As they passed her father's garage, with her house set back some way to one side, Gerry thought again how lucky she was. The Jones family was, she'd decided a long time ago, pretty unique. Maybe because there were only six years between Jeremy, who was the eldest, and herself, they had grown up a very close-knit family. She knew from her classmates that the Jones' rather old-fashioned family life was unusual nowadays. After all, there weren't many families who were all involved in the same type of work. And although things got pretty busy at times, and the hours her parents and brothers put in stretched well past the usual nine-to-five office routine, their family life never suffered. Their very routine gave all of them a sense of belonging, of security.

'Hey! You still awake at the back there?'

Gerry snapped her head round at Clive's question, forgetting her reverie to concentrate on where they were headed. 'Of course I am! Where are we going?' she asked.

'The Moody Cats,' Clive replied, adding, 'Before you ask the obvious, it's a new disco that's opening tonight. A friend of my father's owns it, that's how I managed to get four invites.'

'Oh?' Gerry wasn't sure if she was pleased or not. Discos weren't really her scene – mainly because whenever she got on the floor to dance she somehow couldn't keep in rhythm with the beat.

'Great, don't you think?' Patsie enthused, aware of Gerry's silence.

'Yeah – great,' said Gerry, though even to her ears it sounded flat.

'Don't worry,' Patsie put in. 'It'll probably be so crowded, you won't be expected to actually dance. I know how you hate it – though why, beats me.'

Clive looked at her through the front mirror. 'Don't you like dancing then, Gerry?' he asked, surprised.

Gerry pulled a face at him. 'Well, it's okay,' she allowed. 'The trouble is, I've two left feet and no natural rhythm. And what's more, I can't sing!' She threw that last bit in for laughs and it worked, because Clive's usually serious face creased into a really nice smile.

'Rumour has it you're a whizz kid with wheels though – right?'

Gerry immediately warmed to the subject. 'I enjoy tinkering with cars, yes,' she said brightly. 'Some people think it's a crazy hobby...' she trailed off, wondering if she was making a mistake expecting Clive to be at all interested. Perhaps he was just asking out of politeness. She'd only really got to know him since Patsie introduced them a few weeks before, but he was always nice to her.

Their gazes met again through the driver's mirror.

'Patsie tells me you're building a car, is that right?' His eyes switched to the front as he pulled over to let the car behind them overtake.

'Rebuilding,' Gerry corrected.

He was back with her. 'What is it?'

'An MG,' she replied, then chewed on her bottom lip, wondering why Patsie was giving her a peculiar sideways look.

'MG? They were great little motors. My uncle had one, oh, years ago. I remember seeing photos in the family album – a dark-green J2 model, I think.'

'You're kidding!' Gerry was suddenly wide awake and very excited. 'But that's what I'm rebuilding. He hasn't still got it, has he?'

Clive let out a good-natured laugh. 'Sorry,' he told her. 'He sold it when he got married – said he couldn't afford two fast ladies in his life!'

'Will you two stop being so boring!' Patsie said, making a fuss about settling down in the seat. 'Who's interested in old bangers anyway?'

'Sorry,' said Gerry softly, dropping the subject. But she couldn't help notice Clive glance sharply across at Patsie. For a moment it seemed he was going to say something, but instead he rubbed the side of his temple with a finger and shook his head.

'Women!' he said. It came out lightly and Clive grinned, but Gerry saw that somehow the smile never reached his eyes.

'Who's making up the fourth in the party?' she asked, to change the subject.

'A mate of mine from college,' Clive replied. He swung the car off the main road into a wide, tree-lined avenue where the detached houses were set well back off the road, each flanked with an impressive garden. 'His name's Monte Pollister – but we call him Pole.'

'Why Pole?' Patsie asked, wide-eyed.

'Would you believe because he's nearly six foot two – it's short for Beanpole. Here we are,' he added, swinging the car on to a wide, circular drive which led to a double-fronted, mock Georgian house. It was the type of house you see in advertisements for paints – or in glossy magazines for its splended interior designs, Gerry decided.

Clive got out of the car and went to ring the doorbell, leaving the two girls alone.

'If the guy's anything like his house, he should be pretty impressive!' Patsie said, enviously.

'Oh, come on, don't be like that,' Gerry scolded lightly, not wanting to admit that she too was impressed. 'You shouldn't let material things be important, you know that.'

To Gerry's surprise, her friend spun around in a fury. 'Oh, it's okay for you to talk!' Patsie said.

'What do you mean by that?'

'Just that you live in a lovely house, too – and have a normal family around you. Honestly, you probably take it all for granted, don't you?'

'That's not true, Patsie,' Gerry threw back, hurt by her friend's sudden show of animosity.

'Yeah – well .. look, forget it.' The silence filled the car. Then Patsie said, 'I'm sorry.' She forced a smile. 'It's just that, well – sometimes it's difficult when your parents split up, you know?'

Gerry instinctively reached out and put a comforting hand on Patsie's shoulder. She didn't know – not really. But she could guess. She'd had a good idea of what her friend had been through in the last two years since her mum and dad had split up. The upheaval. Moving from the neighbourhood she'd grown up in, to a flat. Patsie had said it was really for the best. At least her parents didn't row all the time any more. But sometimes, Gerry couldn't help but notice the sad expression shadowing her friend's usually bright, laughing smile.

'I wonder what's taking Clive so long?' Patsie now said, peering through the window, the mood of the moment before forgotten. Or at least, thought Gerry with sudden clarity, pushed behind her friend's sunny smile. She giggled. 'Maybe the Beanpole's mother won't allow her little son to come out to play?'

Gerry nodded. 'Fancy being called, Pole, though. It's not very nice, is it?'

'But very fitting!' Patsie hissed and, following her friend's gaze, Gerry had to admit she was right. Clive, at five foot ten, appeared to be almost dwarfed by his friend as they made their way towards the waiting car.

'He looks like a member of one of those American football teams,' Patsie whispered. 'Hey,' she added, 'do you reckon those shoulders are for real?'

Gerry giggled nervously. 'Have to be,' she said. 'They don't make pads that big, surely?'

'I'd better let him get in the front,' Patsie said, releasing her seat belt and opening the car door. 'If he has to get in the back with you, either you'll have to sit on the floor or he'll have to loop his legs over my shoulders!'

'Stop it!' Gerry spluttered. 'He'll hear!'

'Girls – meet Monte,' Clive said after they'd both clambered into the front. 'Pole – Patsie on the right, and Geraldine on the left.'

'Gerry – please,' Gerry told the newcomer as he smiled at her over his enormous shoulder. 'I hate my full name.'

'Okay – Gerry it is. Hi!' There was a slight lilt to his voice which was really nice, Gerry decided.

'Are you American?' Patsie asked.

'My folks are,' Pole answered. 'I was born in Canada. My dad worked there for a while.' He laughed. 'Come to think of it, my dad has worked nearly every place, for a while. Dad's in oil. So, where the oil is, there's Dad.'

'How long have you been in England?' Gerry asked politely.

'Oh, a long time – for us, that is. It's three years now. But, I should add, my father's still travelling. It's just Mum and me who stopped.'

'Gerry's dad's in oil, too,' Patsie said. 'Isn't he, Gerry?'

'No – well, yes. But not like real oil, if you see what I mean?' Then, to explain herself more clearly, she added, 'Dad's a distributor for domestic oil and some commercial outlets – nothing big, like your father's line, I suppose.'

'Well, the big oil companies have to get rid of their product, which makes men like your father very important – so Dad says,' Pole replied as he turned to smile at Gerry. She smiled back, thinking that he was really good-looking in a clean-cut, all American way. He looked a bit like a younger Ryan O'Neal – only with much blonder hair.

Gerry suddenly realized she wasn't the only one to find their new passenger attractive because, a second later, she felt a sharp kick on her shin. The moment Pole turned round to say something to Clive, Patsie mouthed silently, 'Wow! How about *that*!'

Usually, Gerry would have joined in with Patsie's light-hearted banter. But somehow, studying the thick hair which curled nicely at the nape of Pole's neck, listening to his deep, attractive voice, she didn't feel like sharing in anything. He was really nice. And for the first time since she'd got in the car, Gerry was conscious of how she was dressed and wished she didn't have the bump on her forehead.

Automatically, her fingers reached to examine it. She was relieved to find it had gone down, although the tenderness was still there.

Suddenly she felt Patsie digging her elbows into her ribs. Gerry turned to see what she wanted.

'What's up with you, then?' her friend asked pointedly, keeping her voice just above a whisper. Her usually pretty face was creased with annoyance.

Gerry pointed to her bruised head. 'I banged my head, remember? It's still sore,' she said, as an excuse for being subdued. 'And I've still got a bit of a headache.' It wasn't strictly true, but it was easier than trying to explain her feelings about the boy with the Ryan O'Neal charms.

Far easier, she thought as she looked through the window at the blur of traffic, because to be honest, she wasn't quite sure how she did feel.

Chapter 4

The Moody Cats was a mistake – that was obvious from the moment they arrived. Not that it wasn't beautifully designed – it was. And not that the music wasn't any good. On the contrary, everyone agreed it was great. The trouble was, as Pole remarked after about five minutes, 'The world and his wife have turned up for the grand opening.'

Clive suggested they head off somewhere less 'in' – and more out of town.

'What do you think?' he asked generally, as they edged their way out through the mob that was thronging in.

Everyone agreed it was the best idea so far.

'I'll just go and say hello and goodbye to my dad's friend, if I can find him in there,' Clive said, 'then I'll be right back. Wait for me in the car, okay?' He threw the keys to Pole before heading back into the crowd.

'Looks as if it's going to be a very popular place,' Gerry said, walking between Pole and Patsie to the car.

'Do you like discos?' Pole asked, but before Gerry could reply, Patsie said, 'No, she hates them! She much prefers to be at home with her toy cars.' She giggled, making it into a joke, but somehow Gerry didn't see the funny side of it.

'What toy cars?' Pole asked, puzzled.

Gerry shot Patsie a look which stopped her friend from saying any more.

They'd reached Clive's car before Gerry said, 'I'm interested in a project, that's all.'

'Oh – what kind of project?' Pole opened the rear door and Patsie stood back to let Gerry get in first.

'She's building herself a car, for when she gets her licence in June,' Patsie said with a laugh. 'Daft, eh?'

'Nope! Sounds like a sensible idea to me,' Pole replied.

'Much easier to buy a new one, though,' Patsie said, lingering outside the car after Gerry had already climbed inside.

Gerry chewed on the notion of climbing out again, then thought better of it. Whatever game Patsie was playing, let her get on with it. She really wasn't interested, was she? If Patsie had decided, between starting out for the evening and then meeting Pole, that she preferred her boyfriend's mate, good luck! She just wished she wasn't around to witness it, that's all.

'You sulking in there?' Clive asked, popping his head through the open window on her side a few minutes later.

She wanted to laugh – but somehow it stuck in her throat. So she shook her head.

Clive smiled, then called to the others, who were still chatting outside the car.

They drove to a pizza house Clive knew in the next town, but although Gerry hadn't eaten anything since lunchtime, she wasn't at all hungry.

'You okay?' Clive asked later, as they went to get the car. 'You're very quiet.'

'I bumped my head this afternoon,' Gerry confided, 'and it's still a bit sore. I've got a headache now, too.'

This time it was true. 'I'm afraid I'm not very good company tonight,' she apologized.

They were walking some distance behind Patsie and Pole and as they reached a street lamp, Clive reached out and took her arm.

'Let me see the damage,' he said, pulling her closer, into the glow of the overhead light.

'It's nothing – really.' Gerry began to protest, then stopped as she felt Clive's fingers very gently and tenderly lift her halo of curls off her face.

'Wow! It was quite a knock, wasn't it? What did you do, play football with it?'

She smiled weakly, aware of the concern expressed in Clive's face. 'Sort of. I got up to look at a bolt I'd unfastened – only I forgot I was still under the car.'

Lines of amusement creased the outer edges of Clive's eyes, like rays of sunshine. 'Lesson number one, eh?' he said.

She nodded, but didn't move away from him. Somehow the touch of his fingers, warm and gentle against her skin, was very pleasant. For a second, they just stood and looked into each other's eyes. Then, as if suddenly remembering where they were – and who they were with – he let her go.

'I'll run you home, Gerry,' he said thoughtfully.

'I don't want to break up the party –' she began, but stopped as he shook his head.

'You won't,' he assured her, then added, 'I should get home soon, anyway. I promised Dad I wouldn't have the car out late tonight.'

That seemed reassuring, in a way. To know that he too was involved with 'family'. He reached out and squeezed her hand, then just as quickly let it go.

The news that Clive was driving her home went down like a ton of bricks with Patsie.

'Oh, come on, Gerry! Don't be a spoilsport. It's only eleven o'clock!'

'I've got to get the car back, anyway,' Clive told her. 'And besides, Gerry's not feeling too good.'

Patsie glanced from Gerry to Clive, then looked again. 'What's been going on here, then?' she asked in a singsong tone, implying an intimacy that to Gerry was embarrassing and yet somehow disturbing.

'Nothing's been "going on", Patsie,' Gerry told her friend. 'I did bang my head this afternoon – I told you. And now I've got a bad headache – okay?'

Patsie let out an unsympathetic sigh, then turned her attention to Pole. 'Do you have to be in before lights out, too?' she asked with a pout.

'Nope! So if you like, we could leave these two and I'll see you home later in a cab.'

Gerry glanced away in disgust. How could Patsie do it? Start out the evening with Clive – then leave him for his mate? It was terrible! She felt embarrassed on Clive's behalf, yet she felt she was in some way to blame.

But if Clive was upset, he didn't show any sign of it. All he said was, 'Okay, you guys. If that's how you want it, it's fine by me.'

'You sure, old mate?' Pole asked.

'Of course,' Clive assured him, and to endorse his good feelings he patted his friend on his enormous shoulder.

Gerry gratefully climbed into the front passenger seat of the car, next to Clive. A second later, Patsie poked her face through the open window next to her.

'Enjoy your ride home, Gerry,' she said pointedly, casting a quick, knowing look across to Clive.

Gerry didn't reply. She felt too angry.

'Nice meeting you, Gerry!' Pole called from behind Patsie's head. 'Hope we can meet up again.'

Gerry managed a smile. After all, he seemed nice, even if he had fallen so easily for Patsie's line of patter.

As they drove off, Gerry glanced through the wing mirror and saw Pole slip an easy arm along Patsie's shoulders as they waited to cross the street. Then she caught a glimpse of Patsie laughing up into Pole's face before Clive swung the car off the High Street, heading for her home. But the sight somehow disturbed her and later, as she lay in bed, staring at the shimmering stars outside her window, she tried to analyse, why.

Was she jealous of Patsie, she wondered?

Yes, that could be it. Oh, not of her looks — or anything as silly as that. But the fact was she did envy the easy way Patsie had of making friends. Patsie seemed to find it so easy to chat up boys whereas she — well, she never knew what to talk about except cars, but most times that seemed to put boys off. The trouble was, she was shy. That was stupid really, when she came to think of it, because she was surrounded by boys every day — wasn't she?

Maybe that's what's wrong, she reasoned. It was normal for her to treat her brothers and Mike like — well, like mates. But when it came to the boy — girl bit, she just couldn't handle it.

Take this evening, she thought. She'd liked Pole from the beginning — found him really nice and, yes, attractive. But when it came to the chatting-up part, what did she do? Develop a headache!

And then, when Clive drove her home – quiet, thoughtful Clive – did she stop long enough in the car to thank him properly for going out of his way to drop her off? Oh, no! Not Gerry Jones! The second he'd stopped the car in front of her house, and faced her, what had she done? Smiled sweetly and thanked him with a kiss on his cheek? Not on her life!

'Goodbye,' she'd said, and scrambled out of the car as fast as she could.

Was it any wonder he'd given a little shrug? 'Yeah, well, good night then, Gerry!' he'd called to her retreating figure. Adding, 'See you.' But there'd been a question mark in that statement, indicating that the probability of that happening was nil!

Which, Gerry thought wearily, and with more disappointment than she really understood, was sad, because she really liked Clive. She thumped her pillow, turned on her stomach, and closed her eyes.

She fell asleep almost immediately and dreamt of Clive and Pole in racing cars, chasing her very fast round a circuit. The dream was odd, because as far as she could work out, she was walking! And Patsie was somewhere in the dream – a vague shadow sitting high up in the stands, cheering them all on.

When she woke the next morning, Gerry felt oddly deflated, like a person who had just lost a race. Which was silly, because she hadn't been in a race, had she?

'Bathroom's free, pet,' her mother said, poking her head round Gerry's bedroom door.

'Thanks, Mum.' Gerry swung her long legs out of bed and pulled on her cotton kimono.

'Breakfast in ten minutes, okay?' her mother called back as she ran downstairs.

'Lovely!' Gerry replied.

By the time she'd showered and was dressed in her usual Sunday jeans and sweatshirt, she'd forgotten all about Patsie and Pole, and the night before.

But as she whistled her favourite Paul King single and ran downstairs, towards the tantalizing smells of a cooked breakfast, two things occupied her thoughts. One was the challenge of dismantling the rest of the exhaust – the other was Clive, the boy with the liquid eyes and soft voice whose fingers had touched her face, so gently, the night before . . .

Chapter 5

The garage was closed on Sundays, but that didn't stop Gerry from going out after doing her chores to get on with the job of extricating the good exhaust from its rusted manifold. But just as she was letting herself out through the back door, her mother called her back.

Mary Jones was preparing the regular Sunday roast – some thick ribs of beef which she was rubbing over with seasoning. Beside it was a bowl of potatoes, peeled and ready for the oven.

'What is it, Mum?' Gerry had already helped with peeling the Brussels sprouts and had made up the batter mix for the Yorkshire puddings, so she knew it wasn't to do with helping in the kitchen.

'It's about your homework,' her mother began, and Gerry looked at her, confused.

'What about it?' Gerry was anxious to get on with the car and couldn't understand what her mother was driving at.

'That's just it,' Mrs Jones replied, 'where is it? You were out last night, and I didn't notice you doing any on Friday . . .' she glanced at Gerry as she carried the tin of meat and potatoes to the oven.

'We didn't have any set work to do this weekend,' Gerry explained, relieved that that was all her mother wanted to talk about. She turned to leave, but her mother stopped her.

'Just hold up a second, young lady!' she called, closing the oven door.

Gerry did a quick about-turn. 'But Mum . . .' she began.

'Never mind "But Mum"! As far as I recall, my sweet,' – her mother was facing her now, her arms akimbo – 'you've only got a few weeks before your Mocks, haven't you?'

Gerry nodded; she didn't need to be reminded.

'Then don't you think some revision is more important than an old wreck?' Her mother's left eyebrow arched askance.

'That's not fair!' Gerry exclaimed. 'You know I've never let my hobby get in the way of my school work. That was one of the conditions I've always accepted and so far, I've never got a bad set of marks, have I?'

'Gerry,' – her mother's tone was levelly patient – 'this is slightly different, isn't it? Before, you would have had time to catch up if you slipped behind. This time you're into the exams – well, mock ones at any rate. We've never interfered with your social pastimes before because we know you're a clever girl. But even the most brilliant student has to put in the hours when exams loom.'

Gerry chewed thoughtfully on her bottom lip. 'I know that, Mum,' she said seriously. 'And don't worry, I won't lose out on the exams – honest.'

'Too true honest?' Mrs Jones asked, using her pet phrase for extracting a promise from her children.

'You bet!' Gerry assured her. 'Now,' – she pointed to the door – 'can I go and continue arm wrestling with my toy?'

'You may,' her mother conceded, a little reluctantly.

Gerry didn't need telling twice. She turned and ran – leaving her mother staring after her, half-smiling and shaking her head.

'You staying under there all afternoon, Gerry?' Bobby called. He was crouching down beside the car while Gerry, as usual, was under it. She was down to the last bolt on the exhaust.

'Nearly finished – why?' she called back, making sure she held her head to one side so that there was no repeat of yesterday's mouthful of grit.

'Jeremy's taking his new bike for a spin down to Brighton to see Grandma Jarvis. Sam's studying and I've got a date with a rather lovely blonde I met last night. So he asked if you'd like to ride pillion?'

Gerry stopped what she was doing and peered along to where she could just see her brother's feet, between the gap of the car and the ground. 'You're kidding, Bobby?' she called, her voice tinged with disbelief. Ever since her brother had invested his savings in the brand new Harley Davidson, he'd guarded it as if it were E.T.! No one was allowed even to go near it!

'No kidding. You're very privileged. But you'd better hurry or he might change his mind.'

For a split second, Gerry was torn between getting the last bolt undone and the unique opportunity of a ride on her big brother's bike. 'Tell him I'll be right there!' she called out to Bobby.

'Okay, but don't push your luck. He won't wait.' Gerry watched Bobby's feet disappear into the distance, then eyed the already loosened nut.

Better not, she thought to herself – just in case I get impatient and break the thread. Reluctantly, she scrambled along the ground and out into the warm spring air. She jumped to her feet and pulled off her safety goggles, happy with what she'd already achieved. Impulsively, she plonked a kiss on her greasy hands and placed it fairly and squarely on the rusted chassis of the old MG.

'You may not look too hot, baby,' she said to it, 'but you've got what I want, and I loves you!' Then she ran towards the house.

'Two minutes – no more!' Jeremy called from inside his spanking new leathers – all black and scarlet with silver zips and a shiny matching helmet, which he was in the process of clipping under his chin.

'I'm coming! I'm coming!' Gerry answered, racing through the kitchen past her startled mother to grab a change of clothes.

'And don't forget to pick up the spare helmet on the way out – I'll be in the forecourt.' Jeremy's words followed her in.

'I'll be there!' she called back before disappearing round the banisters and up the stairs; she took them two at a time.

As Gerry ran past her mother on her way out a few minutes later, she felt herself being hauled back.

'Mum! Jeremy won't wait. What is it?' she said, somewhat impatiently.

'You can't go to your gran's looking like that!' her mother exclaimed in horror as she took in Gerry's grubby face and hands.

'I'll keep my helmet on and my hands in my pockets – okay? Now, I must go!' She pulled away, but threw a grin back to her mother. 'Don't worry, Mum, you know how short-sighted Gran is. And besides, she's seen me worse than this on occasions.'

A loud, impatient horn sounding made them both start.

'See you!' Gerry called, escaping through the front door and heading to where her brother sat astride his brand-new Electroglide.

Gerry's breath whistled through her teeth. She'd seen the bike umpteen times before, but it still impressed her with its flashy chrome and gleaming pipes everywhere.

Jeremy made sure she had her helmet on correctly then waited until she was comfortably astride the huge padded seat behind him.

'Hang on – but not too tight. Right?' he shouted to her, and that's exactly what Gerry did. It wasn't the first time she'd ridden pillion with her brothers, but it was the first time on a bike as powerful and smooth as the new Harley Davidson.

Jeremy let the bike slide off its stand and roll down the forecourt towards the road, balancing it with his body and hands. Gerry sat relaxed but straight until, with a throaty cough, the engine kicked into life. She leaned lightly against her brother's back, becoming one with him and the bike as they rode out on to the Brighton road. The wind began to catch at their bodies, whistling past in an airstream as Jeremy opened the throttle and allowed the bike to find its own cruising speed.

It was an incredible feeling. Like flying, Gerry thought. Or swimming like a mighty shark through deep water – smooth, powerful. Fast. She wanted to laugh with happiness, she felt so exhilarated. Thrilled by the feeling of speed and power. And the best thing was that Gerry knew her first ride in her own MG would be even better. She couldn't wait.

It only took twenty minutes to ride to Brighton. Granny Jarvis was pleasantly surprised to see Gerry and her brother, and they spent the next hour chatting away, before beginning the brief journey back home. Gerry thought again of her distant dream – driving herself in her vintage, remodelled MG.

That's if it ever gets finished, she mused. There was so much to do. So much to find. And it wasn't easy. Finding the car had proved to be the easy part. It was tracking down all the necessary spare parts that was difficult.

Jeremy eased down speed as they approached the main set of traffic lights on the High Street before turning off towards their home. The lights were still green, but Jeremy slowed down, to anticipate the change to amber and red. He began to position himself on to the crown of the road, ready to turn right, when an open-topped white sports car suddenly shot out as the lights were changing, and cut dangerously in front of them.

Jeremy applied his brakes by a quick pumping action and the massive bike slid to a smooth halt – only inches from where the back wheels of the sports car cut across them.

Gerry's head spun round. She managed to catch a glimpse of a massive pair of shoulders, a thatch of fair hair and, beside that image, Patsie, her black hair whipped back off her face by the onrush of wind.

By the time Jeremy rode the bike into the forecourt, the incident seemed almost unreal, like a fast-forward on a video. But even so, Gerry was convinced that the dangerous driver of the powerful sports car was Monte – Pole – Pollister. He was obviously on a date with Patsie. Which was their business, Gerry decided. But the fact that they had nearly caused a very serious accident was hers.

She was surprised to find she was shaking like a leaf as she slipped her leg over the seat and dismounted from the bike.

'You okay?' Her brother's voice was like ice. She looked up into his face as he took off his helmet, and saw to her dismay that he too was shaken by the narrow escape.

'I'm fine,' Gerry assured Jeremy, trying to smile and yet failing miserably.

Jeremy wheeled the big bike through to the family garage, then hung both their helmets on pegs on the wall. She stood silently as he unzipped the front of his leather suit and loosened the scarf round his neck.

'Better not tell Mum, kiddo,' he advised. Gerry knew

immediately that he was right. It would be all her mother needed to forbid Gerry ever to ride pillion again. Of course, she'd still let Gerry's brothers go out on the bike, but she would worry even more.

Jeremy slipped an arm round her shoulders and shot her a quick smile. 'You sure you're all right?'

Gerry nodded, reached up and held on to her big brother. Then, arm in arm, they walked into the house. For a second, Gerry was going to ask Jeremy if he had realized it was Patsie in the car – then thought better of it. If he had, he was obviously keeping it to himself. And if he hadn't, then she didn't want to create bad feeling between her brother and her best friend.

'Everything okay, you two?' Mr Jones asked, glancing up from his favourite colour supplement as he relaxed by the television.

'Fine, Dad!' they both chorused.

'Your gran all right, was she?' Gerry's mother asked, after placing a hand to mark the page she'd been reading in her arty flower-arrangement manual.

'Fine,' Gerry told her, flopping on one of the easy chairs, her long, jean-clad legs stuck out in front of her. 'Oh, and Gran sent us back some home-made jam – strawberry, I think.' She giggled, suddenly feeling the tension leaving her limbs. 'Looks like she's going into competition with Granny Jones' marmalade production.'

Mrs Jones shook her head. 'I do hope she isn't,' she said, pulling a pained face. 'Mum never could cook, bless her, though not one of us ever had the heart to tell her.'

'Well, I have to tell you it did look a little runny to

me, and it's rather a peculiar violet shade,' said Gerry, stretching luxuriously.

Her mother rolled her eyes to the ceiling. 'Oh, dear!' she sighed. 'Never mind. We can always donate it to the WI fête in the summer.'

'Mum!' Gerry threw her mother a disgusted look. 'Really!'

'You'd rather eat it?' Her mother's eyes met hers in a challenge. 'Exactly! It goes to the fête, right?'

Gerry shrugged amiably. 'Whatever you say, Mum,' she agreed. 'I'm going up for a shower.'

'Oh, I nearly forgot, pet.' Her mother stopped her in her tracks. 'You had a call.'

'Patsie?' Gerry asked, although that, she quickly realized, wasn't likely in view of the fact that she'd just seen her out with Pole.

'No, actually it was that nice Clive Rowlings. He wanted to know how you were feeling today. Whether your headache had gone.' Her mother smiled, remembering. 'I thanked him for his thoughtfulness. He didn't leave any message, though.'

Gerry felt her cheeks grow hot. 'Oh, didn't he?'

Her mother cocked one quizzical eyebrow as her gaze rested on her daughter's glowing face.

'No, dear. Why? Were you expecting there to be one?' The question, Gerry decided, was loaded. And it made her blush even deeper.

'Not really, no,' she said, as nonchalantly as she could.

Her mother continued to scrutinize her. 'Is Patsie still going out with him, pet?' she now inquired.

Gerry's narrow shoulders shrugged off the question.

45

'Search me!' she said lightly, continuing to leave the room. Then she added, although later she didn't know quite why, 'Anyway it's nothing to me, either way. Patsie's in a world of her own when it comes to dating.' Deciding not to give her mother the time or the opportunity to follow this line of questioning, she slipped out of the room and ran upstairs whistling to herself in a loud carefree kind of way.

Later, Gerry curled up in a chair in her room, her newly washed hair still damp against her forehead and neck from the shower. It had been her second shower of the day, but it had been even more refreshing than the first. She was dressed in a baggy old tracksuit and trainers; her notebook on the rebuilding of the MG lay on her lap; but although she was looking at it, she was thinking about Clive.

Why had he rung her? As far as she recollected, he'd never had her number. She supposed he had simply looked up Jones Garage in the Yellow Pages — the telephone was connected through to the house on Sundays.

Was he just being thoughtful, concerned about her head? More likely he was going to ask if she knew where Patsie was? Yes, that had to be it, she told herself with an odd, deflated feeling. He must have telephoned Patsie's home and when he got no reply, he rang here to see if she was with me. That had to be it. Sunday afternoons, Patsie's mother worked shift at the hospital where she was a receptionist.

Or maybe, because Patsie went off with Pole last night, Gerry suddenly thought, Clive was going to ask me out to make her jealous . . . !

Well, I wouldn't have gone, she thought defiantly. Not under those circumstances. No way.

She forced herself to concentrate on checking off the spare parts she still needed. The list was very long – and expensive, if she wasn't lucky. So far, between her brothers' and Mike's scrap-hunting, it hadn't been too bad.

The knock-on wire wheels would be a biggy, she mused, chewing the end of her pencil. And she'd need a twelve-gallon petrol tank, with a dipstick because the one on the old chassis was rusted right through . . .

You would have gone out with him, a small voice suddenly piped up inside her, overriding her efforts to concentrate on the handwritten list before her eyes. She shook her head, trying to dismiss her errant thoughts. Finally she gave up and dropped the pencil she'd been holding into the spine of the book before closing it with a snap.

It was all too confusing even to think about. Up to last night she'd never bothered about boys, or about dating – not like Patsie, or many of her other friends in her class.

A sigh escaped her lips. Now look what had happened. In one evening, she had been attracted first to Clive's friend, Pole – and then to Clive!

She deliberated that thought in her mind for a while. Surely she was behaving in a rather fickle way? Mentally she again visualized the two boys – one so tall and fair, the other not so tall, dark and with liquid brown eyes.

Had she been attracted to Pole only because she'd known that Clive belonged to Patsie? Or had she been drawn to Clive, as the evening wore on, because of

Patsie's behaviour? Maybe she'd felt sorry for Clive because of the position Patsie had put him in?

Gerry shook her head. It was all far too confusing. It was much easier to deal with cars. Determined not to let it bother her any further, she went in search of her brothers. A few minutes later, she was deep in a fascinating conversation with Sam – discussing the best way of tackling the rusted running boards he'd picked up for her in a junk yard on one of his foraging expeditions.

They were still talking animatedly when Mrs Jones called them down for a late Sunday dinner.

Chapter 6

On Monday, Patsie came running across the playground as Gerry walked through the gates. Her pretty face was flushed, her dark eyes flashing.

'Hi, Gerry! You're late! I've been waiting for you.'

Gerry glanced at her watch. It was only twenty to nine. 'It's not me who's late,' she said, as her friend slipped an arm through hers, 'you must have been up at the crack of dawn.'

Patsie pulled her arm free and gave Gerry a playful shove. 'There you go again, always contradicting me. Why do you always have to be right, anyway?'

It was said in a light-hearted way and Gerry, grinning, said, 'Because I always am, remember? You're the one with the good looks – I've got the brains!'

A couple of other friends came over to join them –

Sandy, a thin, studious-looking girl with glasses and a quick, easy smile and Miranda, an exotic-looking girl whose parents had come to England from Cyprus.

'Guess what?' Patsie said to the assembled huddle.

Gerry had some idea what was coming, but even so, Patsie's announcement was still a bit of a shock.

'I've got the most smashing, hunky new boyfriend you've ever seen!' Patsie enthused. She turned to Gerry. 'Go on, tell them it's true, Gerry-baby! Isn't Monte something else?'

Sandy and Miranda were all ears.

'What about Clive Rowlings?' Gerry asked, instead.

Patsie pulled a face. 'Oh, he's okay – but he's a bit serious – you know, like b-o-r-i-n-g,' she said, making a great point of drawing out the word and rolling her eyes to the heavens. 'But Monte – well . . .' she didn't need to continue with her description, her facial expression left no doubt in any of the girls' minds just how gorgeous he was.

'Don't you call him Pole, then?' Gerry asked, detaching herself from Patsie's clasp and starting to walk towards the main building.

'No. Of course not. That's for the others. To me, he's Monte.' She sighed happily. 'Isn't it unusual, eh?' She turned to the other girls, who had fallen into step with Gerry. 'We met him on Saturday, didn't we, Gerry? He's at the Technical College with Clive.' She giggled. 'Trust old Clive to keep someone like Monte quiet – can't stand the competition, if you ask me.'

'Hey! That's not fair!' Gerry suddenly put in. 'It was Clive who introduced you, remember?'

There must have been an edge to her voice, because Patsie stopped walking to confront her. 'Wait a second, there,' she said, narrowing her eyes to scrutinize her friend. 'What's this I hear? Why so jumpy? What's Clive to you, anyway?' Then, before Gerry could reply, Patsie asked, 'Did something happen after you two drove off into the sunset?'

'Don't be silly!' Gerry dismissed the implication with a shrug. But Patsie wouldn't let it go. She skipped along backwards, in front of Gerry.

'Go on, Gerry. Tell all! Did he kiss you, then?'

It was Miranda who came to the rescue. 'Lay off, Patsie!' she said. 'From what you've just told us, what Clive does from here on is none of your concern anyway.'

'That's right!' Sandy agreed.

'But of course it's my concern,' Patsie insisted. 'After all, just because I've got Monte doesn't mean I'm not interested in Clive. Clive's still very nice – even if he is boring. And besides, Gerry's my best mate and what concerns her concerns me. I've your best interests at heart, haven't I, Gerry-baby? I'm the one who looks after you.'

Gerry felt as if she was being got at – in a bantering sort of way. For a moment, she wanted to tell her friend that she didn't need to be looked after. In fact, she would be delighted if Patsie dropped her from her social list completely, outside school. Sometimes she wondered why she stayed best friends with Patsie. But just then, the bell rang for school to start. So all she said was, 'Patsie – stop calling me Gerry-baby, will you?'

Later, Gerry was relieved she hadn't had a confrontation with Patsie because when it came to it, she realized that her friend, in her own way, really did have her best interests at heart. She also realized that, despite Patsie's generally voiced opinion that Gerry needed her, it was really the other way round. Patsie needed her more than ever since her parents had divorced.

It was lunchtime before Patsie again brought up the subject of Clive. Only this time, with just the two of them walking round the perimeter of the playing fields after their school meal, she was more subdued.

'You mad at me?' she asked her friend, glancing at her through narrowed lids.

'Why do you ask?' Gerry wasn't going to let her get off the hook that easily.

'You are, aren't you? And it's about Clive – I mean,' she corrected herself, 'about my teasing you about him? I didn't mean to.'

Gerry didn't reply, just cast her a quizzical look.

Patsie pinked, glanced away, then, hands deep inside her pockets, she hugged her school blazer tighter round her body. 'Well, I'm sorry if you took it the wrong way.'

'It doesn't matter.' Gerry stopped abruptly and faced the taller girl. 'Tell me one thing,' she said.

A guarded look came over Patsie's face as she tossed her hair back over her shoulder. 'You sound pretty serious – what is it?'

'It *is* serious,' Gerry replied, looking at Patsie directly.

'Shoot, then.'

'Were you with Pole – I mean Monte – yesterday afternoon in a white sports car?'

Expressions of at first confusion, then surprise chased across Patsie's face in quick succession. 'Yes – but how did you know . . .?'

'You nearly caused Jeremy and me to come off his motorbike, that's how!' Gerry informed her amazed friend. 'You shot the lights at the High Street. Jeremy only just managed to stop in time. It was a very scary five seconds,' she finished.

Patsie nodded slowly, her face suddenly pale. 'I didn't know that was you,' she said. 'Honestly, I told Monte to wait, but I think he wanted to show off. We'd been for a ride in the country. He bought me a smashing meal in a pub in the village – oh, I forget the name.' She was quite animated as she recalled her date, then her animation instantly died as she saw the look in Gerry's eyes. 'Well, he drank too much beer – but I did tell him, honestly. He didn't mean any harm . . .'

Gerry let out her breath sharply, but didn't say a word. What had come over her friend lately? She wasn't normally this irresponsible.

Patsie took her hands from her pockets and readjusted the golden slide which held her long hair off her face.

'I'm sorry,' she said, after a while.

As a reply, Gerry asked, 'I hope you know what you're doing, Patsie. You don't need me to tell you how fatal it can be for someone to drink and drive. Especially in a powerful car like the one Monte was driving.'

A ghost of a smile flitted over Patsie's face, then vanished. 'You can say that again!' she said. 'Next time, though, I'll refuse to let him drive me home. The trouble is, you know how I hate walking.'

Gerry had to smile at the pained look on her face at the thought of actually having to walk. 'You could always ring our garage,' she suggested. 'We've a twenty-four-hour pick-up service, you know.'

'For cars – not for girls, nut!' Patsie said, happy that her friend's serious mood was lightening.

'Look, Patsie – all my three brothers would be more than happy to turn out for you if you were in trouble.'

'You've got to be kidding?'

Gerry shook her head. 'I'm not,' she said. Then, grinning, 'I reckon they all fancy you, you know?'

Patsie's bubbling personality was back on form. 'Is that for real? Wow!'

'You want it in writing?'

Patsie linked an arm through Gerry's, smiling brightly. 'Well, I've got my hands full at present – with my Canadian friend. But if that ever peters out, I'll bear in mind what you just confided to me. And while we're talking about sharing confidences, I reckon Clive Rowlings fancies you, too.' She glanced casually across at Gerry. 'That's if you're in the least bit interested,' she said, ending with, 'which, of course, I know you're not.'

Gerry frowned. 'Who says he is?'

'I do. Ever since I introduced you to him, he was forever asking me to invite you to tag along. So – what do you make of that?'

'I think you're making more of it than there is,' Gerry announced.

The two girls reached the end of the playing fields and stopped to watch the school's hockey team, practising on the last field. After a while, they turned and made their way back towards the school buildings.

It wasn't until they were walking into the main building that Gerry broke their companionable silence.

'Did you give Clive my number?' she inquired, as

nonchalantly as she could.

Her friend shook her head, her ponytail dancing a tango down her back. 'Nope! Why, don't tell me he rang you?'

Gerry tried not to smile, but the telltale twinkle in her deep-blue eyes gave her away. 'He might have,' she said.

Patsie wasn't being put off. 'Why, you sly old thingy!' she cried. 'Go on, what did he say?'

'Nothing,' replied Gerry, stringing her friend along.

A hand shot out and stopped Gerry's progress along the corridor. 'How come – nothing? He must have said something?' Patsie insisted.

'Not to me he didn't.' Gerry poked her tongue out at her friend. 'I was out – see!'

'So didn't you ring him back?' Her friend sounded incredulous.

'No – of course not.'

'Why not?'

Gerry tried to remember, then shrugged. 'I forgot,' she said, telling half the truth.

'Come on – tell me another! You were shy, right?'

It was true, but there was no way Gerry was going to admit it. Not even to her closest friend.

'I got talking to Sam about my project,' she said, which was true – although if she were honest she would admit that she only went to talk to Sam to stop herself thinking about her jumbled emotions. 'And then it was supper time . . .' she ended, studying her feet to avoid looking directly into Patsie's inquisitive eyes.

The bell rang for afternoon school and the two friends ran along the rest of the corridor to their form room to get their books ready for their first lessons. Patsie had Home Economics; Gerry, Maths.

'See you later!' Gerry called as they parted company.

'Not today,' Patsie called back, happily. 'Monte's picking me up straight from school. We're going to the cinema, as Mum's on duty.'

'Well – drive carefully then.' Gerry was serious.

'I'll make sure, don't worry. And you should be daring, for once, and ring Clive!'

'I thought you said he was boring?' Gerry reminded her.

'I was lying, okay? And besides, even if he were, he'd be a heck more exciting than your model car Lego kit!'

Gerry didn't bother to answer her friend's comment. She'd given up months ago trying to explain to Patsie how much enjoyment she derived from a project like rebuilding a vintage car.

But then most people, Gerry had found, weren't really interested in what went on under a car's bonnet, let alone any other aspect of car-building.

In fact, she'd been quite surprised to discover that Clive had shown an interest in her hobby. During their brief conversation in the car, he'd seemed almost enthusiastic. And she'd been really thrilled to know that his uncle had actually owned an original J2 model.

Now that had really interested her . . .

She sat through a Maths revision class and came out, forty minutes later, realizing with a start that she hadn't heard anything the Maths master had said. She'd spent the entire time staring through the window, thinking about the boy who supposedly didn't mean anything to her!

Making a mental note to do extra revision at home

to make up for the wasted lesson, she packed her books into her school bag, then ran to catch up with Miranda and Sandy. Together, the three friends walked to the bus stop, Gerry only half-listening to her friends as they discussed the latest hit album. In the distance, they saw Patsie drive off in Monte's white sports car. The other girls were quite impressed with the car and made a big fuss, but Gerry was too involved with her thoughts of Clive to take any notice. Perhaps he'd read her mind, she thought later, because as soon as she arrived home, the telephone rang.

Chapter 7

What did a bright, sophisticated girl say when a boy asked her for a date? Gerry wished she knew, because she was sure she'd really screwed things up.

'Hi!' Clive had said. 'How are you today?'

Her smart reply? 'Fine.'

You could hardly blame a boy if he went a bit silent after that abrupt answer, she thought afterwards, wanting to kick herself.

'I rang yesterday, but you weren't home.'

Did she say, 'Thank you', or 'No, sorry, I was out with my brother visiting my gran'? Like heck she did. She just said, 'That's right!' – which sounded either as if he was a moron, or she was telling him it was none of his business. Either way, she'd fouled things up.

The trouble was, she was so nervous that she'd

found it difficult to talk at all.

'Look, I was wondering if you'd like to come over and meet Uncle Ted next Sunday?' Clive said, breaking the silence. 'He's the one who had the MG, remember? He's a great *aficionado* of old cars – you'd have a lot in common. Trouble is, he doesn't come down often. He lives in Yorkshire. But he's down for some sales conference and is staying the weekend. So, what do you think?'

Gerry had wanted to say she'd be thrilled – for many reasons. But it seemed she couldn't help acting like a ninny as she heard herself say flatly, 'That would be very nice. Thank you.' The type of reply you'd give to someone offering you a seat in a bus. A polite, unemotional response to a stranger. It was hardly the type of reply a girl should give a boy who was asking her for a date. Her very first date!

Still, it didn't seem to put him off arranging to pick her up at three the following Sunday afternoon. Although, Gerry thought after he'd rung off, maybe he'd only said that to get off the phone? Her throat was still dry and her hand, where it had been clutching the receiver, was damp and clammy.

She'd convinced herself that by Sunday he would phone to cancel the whole deal! Well, she sighed despondently, so what? At least, if that happened, she'd have all Sunday to get on with the car. But oddly, for once, the idea didn't weave its usual spell. Not that she had time to ponder too much, because her mother was calling her – and she didn't need two guesses why. Mondays were her mother's flower-arranging evenings, when Gerry took over the kitchen. She didn't have to do very much, other than serve up what was already prepared – usually a combination dish using up Sunday's leftovers.

'Rissoles and red cabbage tonight, pet,' Mary Jones told Gerry, untying her apron and walking round the table to take a quick look inside the eye-level oven. 'And there's baked apples to follow. It's all timed for seven-thirty – okay?'

'Okay!' Gerry replied, smiling broadly, which seemed to surprise her mother.

'What happened?' Mrs Jones asked, a furrow between her brows. 'You look like the cat who got a whole gallon of cream! No groans about serving supper for once?'

Gerry avoided her suspicious gaze. 'I don't know what you mean?' She suddenly got very busy filling a glass with water.

'No?' her mother asked, with a wide grin. 'Nothing to do with that telephone call you just had, I suppose?' Then, to Gerry's surprise, she added, 'Who was it? Clive Rowlings?'

Gerry's mouth dropped open. 'How...?' she began, then stopped as she saw her mother's amused gaze.

'I'm not a clairvoyant, pet,' she assured her startled daughter. 'It's just that he rang earlier. I told him to ring around five, when you'd be home.'

Gerry's cheeks were flaming. 'He's asked me to go and meet his uncle,' she confessed. Then added quickly – very quickly, 'On Sunday because his uncle lives in Yorkshire and doesn't come down very often and he used to own an MG J2!' It all came out in a rush, the words jumbled together, as though explaining the bit about the MG threw a different light on the whole episode, making what might appear to be a date nothing more than an educational expedition!

Gerry drew in a breath, then glanced across to see what effect this news had had. To her surprise her mother didn't seem unduly concerned.

'That'll be nice, pet,' she said and walked out of the kitchen as Gerry stared, open-mouthed.

She decided not to tell Patsie about Clive telephoning. In fact, she decided not to tell Patsie about her date on the coming Sunday, either. Not particularly because she wanted to hide anything from her best friend, but mainly because if Clive did ring to cancel after her unenthusiastic acceptance, she wouldn't be put in the embarrassing position of having to tell Patsie that she wouldn't be going, after all.

But to Gerry's surprise, by Saturday, Clive still hadn't rung to change their plans. Mind you, Gerry reminded herself on Saturday evening as she lay in the bath, there was still time! She turned the hot tap off, then lay back, letting the softly scented water lap over her, removing the grime of another good day's work.

She was really pleased with the progress she was making on the car. The exhaust had proved to be in excellent condition. She'd spent a long time cleaning, then polishing it until the steel gleamed like new.

'That's quite a find,' Sam had remarked, poking his head round the door of the Tin Barn while she was adding the final touches with a fluffy, soft cloth. 'It's in perfect nick!'

Gerry stood back to admire the gleaming exhaust which had cost her so much time – and patience – as well as a bump on her head which was now thankfully only a memory.

'What's next?' her brother asked.

'I'm not sure,' she confessed. 'Mike said he'd look over the engine with me just to make sure it's sound. But I'm sure it is. I couldn't see any cracks in the block, or head – '

'Hark at you!' Sam teased. 'Where d'you pick up that technical jargon from, then?'

'From you, of course! And Pa, and Jeremy and Bobby! What do you think I grew up with round you lot? Most kids grow up listening to nursery rhymes or lullabies, all I ever heard was talk about clutch linings and carburetters, so what do you expect?'

Sam burst out laughing. 'You've got a point there, sis,' he agreed. Then he added, 'But I'm sure I read somewhere that girls were supposed to play with dolls, and like dressing up in pretty clothes . . .'

'Get o-u-t!' Gerry had turned her brother round and shoved him through the door of the Tin Barn.

'Hey – ' he began, but then thought better of it. Gerry in a temper was a match for any of them!

Now, smiling as she remembered, Gerry sat up and lathered the big bath sponge. Then she stretched out and began leisurely to wash her long, shapely legs, her flat stomach, and tight, neat bottom. She pulled her hair away from her neck with one hand and lathered over her shoulders, round her neck, then her breasts. As she stood up to reach the shampoo by the sink, she caught a glimpse of herself reflected in the misted bathroom mirror. She stopped, and for the first time appraised herself as a woman.

'Not bad,' she decided, saying the words aloud, as if

to assure herself. True, she wasn't as well formed as Patsie, or as pretty, but in her own, willowy way she looked – well – okay.

'Very okay!' she corrected herself, then giggled and plunged back down into the warm, foaming water, sending a spray of bubbles over the bath to frost the pink fitted carpet.

After a quick delve through her wardrobe, Gerry decided on her denim skirt, blue and white checked shirt, and cowboy boots to wear on Sunday. The skirt was the latest length and came over the top of her boots. She'd chosen it because it was trimmed at the waistband with leather, which matched her good boots. She left the top two buttons of the crisp blouse undone, then pulled up the collar at the back, allowing her hair to fall over it, down to her shoulders. A touch of lip gloss and the merest hint of sapphire eye-shadow completed the natural look.

She was about to take a last look at 'La Image' when she heard a car draw up in the forecourt. Running over, she peered through the nets – and there he was!

For a split second, she thought she was going to pass out with panic. How could she ever have agreed to this? The next moment, her mother was calling her downstairs. When she ran down, Clive was already shaking hands with her father, and Sam was smiling at him.

'Hey – you're at the Tech, too, now I come to think of it,' her brother was saying.

'Advanced Engineering,' Clive replied. 'You?'

'Mechanics – first year,' Gerry's brother informed her date.

Her date! It sounded so – well, formal and quaint. Just the thought of it made Gerry want to giggle – or was that nerves?

'Hi!' she greeted Clive. 'I see you've met some of the family already.'

She felt his eyes run over her, then he smiled. Did he like how she looked? She lowered her eyes, but not before noticing he'd made an effort to look good, too. He wore a pair of well-pressed cream cords, topped with a camel polo-neck jumper. It went fantastically with his dark hair.

'We won't be late back,' Clive now informed her folks.

'How much would you take to keep her?' That was Jeremy, who'd come in from the garage. He stuck out a greasy hand, then withdrew it. 'Sorry about that – we'll shake another time. I'm up to my elbows in sump at the moment.'

Clive smiled. 'Trouble with your motor?'

'No – just keeping my bike well lubricated,' he explained.

Gerry got the impression they could have continued with the conversation, but her mother reminded everyone that Clive was there to pick up Gerry, not to have a general discussion.

'Hope we meet again,' Sam said, as they all saw the pair off.

'I hope so, too,' Clive said warmly, stepping out of the door. 'You've got another brother, haven't you?' he asked Gerry as he walked her to the car.

Gerry nodded. 'Bobby. He's dating a girl he met bowling last week. It has to be serious, he's been out with her twice!' A smile lit her glowing face.

Clive studied her. 'I like that,' he said.

Puzzled, she said, 'What? Bobby dating his new girlfriend twice?'

'Nope. You, when you smile.'

Compliments were new to Gerry – from boys, at least. Her brothers had spent a lifetime teasing her about the way she looked. Now, shy and embarrassed, she was glad that Clive had opened the passenger seat door for her, and quickly she clambered inside.

She wasn't really nervous in the car, alone with him. Not after a while, at least. Mainly because he was so relaxed and talked about things she felt at home with. Like cars – and racing . . .

She was delighted to find that he knew even more about the racing scene than Bobby, who followed it very seriously. He also seemed to know about custom cars, Sam's area. When she got on to Jeremy's passion, motorbikes, he confessed to owning a Triumph Bonneville.

'Not that I get to ride her to her full capacity on British roads, of course,' he told her. 'But I went with some mates last summer to Germany and there I opened her up to a hundred and twenty most of the time. She doesn't look like a very impressive machine, but she's very powerful.'

He smiled across at Gerry. 'You know, this is very refreshing,' he told her, a new softness in his voice.

Gerry was puzzled. 'What is?'

'Talking like this – with a girl,' he told her.

'Oh?' His look and the tone of his voice had the effect of making her throat and mouth dry up.

'Yeah. I mean there aren't many girls you can talk to about motor racing, and cars and bikes . . .' he paused and looked at her briefly again. 'Don't go thinking it's a put-off, Gerry,' he said, sincerely. 'On the contrary, I think it's great!'

'You do?' She wanted to tell him that on the few occasions she'd brought up the topic with the double dates Patsie had lined up for her, most of the boys had looked at her as if she were a weirdo – or worse!

'I guess,' Clive said, glancing in the wing mirror as a motorbike overtook them, 'it's good to be with someone you have something in common with. Especially if that someone is pretty and bright.'

This comment made her very self-conscious. 'What do you think of Alain Prost?' she said, changing the line of conversation. 'Don't you think he's got as much racing style as Nikki Lauda?'

She felt Clive take her measure with puzzled eyes. Then he went back to concentrating on the road ahead.

'Well, that is a question for debate,' he answered, a smile playing around the corners of his lips.

Gerry guessed that he'd understood her reason for turning the conversation away from herself. And that embarrassed her even more.

'He's a great world champion,' she gamely continued, avoiding Clive's series of quick glances, 'but Bobby thinks René Arnaud is a likely challenger.' She stopped to draw breath, then asked, 'What do you think?'

'I think you're being unnecessarily nervous and there's no need to be, because my folks and Uncle Ted are very easy to get on with – okay?'

That made her laugh. He obviously didn't realize that her nervousness had nothing to do with either his parents – or his Uncle Ted. It was being so close to him that was making her gabble like a demented idiot. And she'd convinced herself she was going to be cool and clever and witty, like Patsie. Ha!

Now, she chewed thoughtfully on her bottom lip and stared through the windscreen, wondering how she was ever going to survive the whole afternoon without looking like a prize nerd.

But as it was, after Clive parked the car and walked her round the back of his parents' semi to join his mother, father and uncle, who were in the garden, she soon discovered he hadn't exaggerated. Within five minutes she found herself happily relaxed, chatting away about her favourite subject, as if they'd all known each other for years.

It was uncanny, strange – but it was, she decided, a great feeling!

Chapter 8

There was a definite family likeness between Clive and his uncle, Gerry decided. Even more than between him and his own father. If anything, Clive had slightly darker colouring, but he had the same tight curly hair and strong, square jawline and they both had deep clefts in their chins. Unlike Clive, however, his Uncle Ted turned out to be very gregarious and never seemed to let the conversation die for long.

After they'd had a long discussion about the MG he used to own, and about her own ambitious plans to rebuild a working model, Clive's mother suggested they all go indoors for tea. It was a welcome suggestion, as the warmth had gone from the afternoon sun. But Gerry was surprised at the assumption that she would be staying for tea.

'But my dear, it's all arranged. Didn't Clive explain?' Clive's mother shook her head at her son. 'Sometimes, I'm convinced he lives in a different world.' She put a hand on Gerry's arm and led her into the house.

'Sunday afternoons are a ritual in this house, Gerry,' Clive's father explained. 'It's an excuse for my wife to show off her cake-making. We always have a proper, sit-down affair, so don't go thinking it's just for your benefit.' He smiled warmly, then pointed to the sofa. 'Sit yourself down while I go and make myself useful.'

'Can't I help?' Gerry offered, remembering her manners. But her offer was waved aside.

'You stay and chat some more with Ted. I'm sure you'd enjoy it far more – both of you.'

'Well, I know I will,' Uncle Ted announced, sitting in one of the easy chairs opposite Gerry. 'Now, what colour are you thinking of doing the respray when you get her finished?' he asked, enthusiasm filling his voice. Then he added, 'Red, I'd guess. Women always seem attracted to red cars.'

Gerry shook her head, then told him she preferred green.

'British Racing Green, of course?' Clive put in.

'Of course!' Gerry replied, grinning.

His uncle nodded in agreement. 'Great! Really authentic, eh? I hope you'll invite me down for the grand unveiling – when you take her out for her first spin?'

'I'd be delighted if you'd join me on her first road test,' Gerry offered. She really liked Ted Rowlings and thought it fantastic to find someone as enthusiastic about her project as she was.

'Hey, wait a sec – I'm first in the queue!' Clive cut in on their conversation.

'We'll see about that – ' his uncle replied with a grin, but any further discussion was squashed when Mr Rowlings entered, carrying a tray piled high with cups, saucers and plates. Behind him, carrying another tray simply groaning with sandwiches, biscuits and home-made cakes, came his wife.

'Match adjourned until after our tea break!' Ted Rowlings announced, standing up and following his brother and sister-in-law to the table.

It was nearly eight by the time Gerry insisted she had to go home.

Mr and Mrs Rowlings saw her and Clive to the door, while Uncle Ted accompanied them all the way to the car.

'Do come again, Gerry!' Mrs Rowlings called, waving across the small expanse of lawn, edged with a profusion of colourful spring flowers.

'Yes, thank you. It's been lovely!' Gerry called back.

'And remember what I told you, young lady,' Ted Rowlings reminded her as she climbed in the car. 'If you get stuck for any spare parts, just let me know. That friend I sold mine to is still in the car business, and he might be able to help.' He carefully closed her door for her.

Gerry smiled her thanks. 'I won't forget,' she promised, as Clive put the car into gear. She waved to the Rowlings again and called 'Goodbye' through the open window, then they drove home in companionable silence.

When Clive stopped the car in front of the Jones' house a few minutes later, Gerry suddenly didn't know what to say.

'Would you like to come in for a coffee –' she began hesitantly, wanting him to say yes, yet hoping he'd say no, so that the nervous trembling in her stomach would go away.

'Thanks – but no thanks,' he told her, regarding her rather seriously.

Disappointment and relief chased around Gerry's fuddled brain. She had a feeling that the whole afternoon was merely a formality, leading up to this second in her life.

Help! What was she supposed to do? Would he kiss her? Should she kiss him? Patsie – what would Patsie do? Gerry thought frantically.

Clive didn't make a move, which was even more disturbing than if he'd suddenly leaned forward and taken her in his arms, she decided.

'It's been great,' he finally said, still studying her face.

She nodded, smiled breezily, then began to feel for the door handle.

'Here, let me.' In one smooth movement, he leaned forward to unlatch the door but before he let it swing open, his other hand slid along the back of her seat.

'Gerry?'

She turned at the sound of her name, so soft on his lips. Then she discovered, to her quickly mounting excitement, that somehow his lips were pressing very, very gently on hers.

Before she could even think what she ought to do next, he moved away and, behind her, she heard the car door swing open. A rush of cold air brought her back to reality.

'Good night, Gerry,' he said, smiling at her again as if nothing had happened. As if his lips hadn't just tenderly touched hers.

She scrambled from the car, then stood dazed for a moment before she shut the door. 'Good night,' she called, her voice strangely distant and husky. Unconsciously, the fingers of her left hand crept up to touch her lips while she waved him off with her right hand.

'Good night' ... she whispered the words through her fingertips, feeling in her mind his lips on hers: the soft and gentle pressure. It was strange, unlike anything she'd ever experienced – ever dreamed of. She grinned suddenly, then giggled. Still bubbling with happiness, she hurried across the garage forecourt towards the amber lights which shone like miniature beacons from the windows of her home.

Gerry thought she'd get at least one call from Clive during the following week, but although she ran to answer the phone whenever she heard it ring, none of the callers was Clive.

On Friday, she let slip to Patsie that she'd been round to his house.

'And you never told me? Why, you rotten moo!' she retorted, pouting in mock annoyance. 'I always tell you everything about my love life!'

'I haven't got a love life, silly!' Gerry was quick to correct any misconceptions her friend may have dreamed up.

'Not yet!' Patsie said, then shut up as she saw the stern look on Gerry's face.

'I was only invited to meet Clive's uncle because he's an MG specialist,' she said, simply trying to subdue her friend's enthusiasm. Yet could it be true? Perhaps Clive hadn't considered her visit on Sunday a real date, and that's why he hadn't called. But he had kissed her . . .

Patsie pulled a face. 'Oh, right! Of course. It wasn't anything serious, like Clive fancying you, was it?'

Maybe because she was upset at not hearing from Clive, Gerry nearly lost her temper with her friend. 'Can't you think of anything but boys, boys, boys?' she exploded, before storming off across the playing field – leaving Patsie wide-eyed with surprise and anger.

After school, Gerry made a point of finding her friend and apologizing for her outburst. She knew she'd over-reacted.

Patsie wasn't giving in that easily, though. 'Forget it, Gerry,' she said dismissively, as she looked at her wristwatch. She made a show of glancing up and down the road. Then she let out a sigh, and finally turned to Gerry. 'Look, in future, just don't take it out on me if your particular path of true love has a few bumps in it, okay?'

Gerry was going to say Patsie was wrong – but at that moment Monte's car appeared on the scene.

'Hey! Gerry! Can I give you a lift somewhere?' he called across to her, but before she could refuse, Patsie turned and gave her a 'hands-off' glare.

'Er – thanks – but I'm going in the opposite direction

tonight,' Gerry said.

'What direction's that?' Monte asked. 'You going to visit poor old Clive in his sick bed?'

His words made Gerry stop and turn back. She walked to the side of the car, and leaned down so that her face was level with Monte's.

'I didn't know he *was* sick,' she said.

Surprise filled the handsome, freckled face. 'Oh? I got the impression from him on Monday that you two . . .' he trailed off, seeing the expression on her face. Then he added, 'He's got chickenpox, poor bloke. Since Tuesday. Highly contagious, so you'd best stay away. A couple of other guys in the college have gone down with it.'

So that explained why she hadn't had a call from him! With a sigh of relief and a soaring heart, Gerry made her way to the bus stop. Then, on an impulse, she decided to buy a 'get well' card from the newsagent's on the shopping parade.

The card she eventually decided on wasn't smart, or clever, nor was it romantic. It was a cartoon drawing of a bandaged car with a sticking plaster on its bonnet. Inside was written: *Hope You'll Be on The Road Again Soon*!

Once she got home, she deliberated over what she should write inside. Should she sign 'with love' – or 'with warmest wishes'? No, the first was too pushy, and the second too formal. In the end she just signed 'Gerry', then added 'Jones' – then wished she hadn't! She then realized she didn't have his address. After more deliberation, Gerry rang Patsie, only to find that Patsie wasn't home.

'She's out, Gerry,' Patsie's mother told her, adding,

her tone puzzled, 'but I thought she was going with you and some other girls from school to do some swotting for the exams?'

Caught off-guard, Gerry mumbled that she wasn't able to make it – then asked if, by any chance, she knew Clive's address.

'Clive Rowlings? Yes, I'm sure Patsie wrote it down in our address book. She has all her friends' addresses in it. Hang on.'

A minute later, she gave Gerry Clive's address. She still didn't sound at all happy.

Gerry rang off and let out an annoyed sigh. She had assumed that Monte had simply given her friend a lift home. As she wandered back to her room to write out the address on Clive's card she wondered just what Patsie was up to. It wasn't the first time she'd been used as a cover. But it will be the last, Gerry decided, licking the envelope of Clive's card, then sealing it. Tomorrow, she'd have it out with Patsie! Meanwhile, she got a stamp from her mother, then ran down the road to post the card before the evening collection.

On the way back, she wondered if she'd done the right thing. Was she being too enthusiastic? Showing too much concern, too soon? Assuming a closer friendship than there really was?

But he had kissed her... she reminded herself again.

Gerry blushed slightly, remembering the sensation. As she cut across the garage forecourt she almost bumped into Mike, who was just coming off duty.

'Better hurry, Gerry!' Mike said as she sidestepped to avoid crashing into him. 'Your brother Jeremy's got some good news for you!'

'What is it?' she asked in anticipation.

'Wait and see!' Mike replied, then waved goodnight.

Patience wasn't one of Gerry's virtues, so against 'house rules' she sprinted across to the office, which was above the service station, then ran up to where Jeremy was still working.

Her brother was sitting in front of a small computer her father had installed to handle the accounts. Knowing better than to interrupt him when he was feeding in data, she plonked herself on one of the swivel seats and began to spin herself round, faster and faster.

'You got a licence for doing that?' her father called from the doorway, a scowl on his face.

Gerry stopped herself abruptly. 'Sor-ry!' she said, in a singsong fashion.

'So what are you doing up here?' her father inquired, crossing the room to confront her. 'Something urgent that couldn't wait till dinner?'

Gerry shook her head and stood up. 'No, it's just that Mike said Jeremy had something for me and as I was on my way in, I just thought – '

Her father was shaking his head at her. Knowing she was in the wrong, she stood up and began to sidestep towards the door. After all, business was business and she was aware that for someone who had only just finished his business manager's course, Jeremy carried a lot of responsibility and shouldn't be bothered.

Just as she was about to slip through the door, Jeremy finished at the computer.

'It's okay, kid.' He beckoned her back. 'I was just packing up here anyway. Look,' – he handed her a piece of headed paper – 'I thought you might be interested in this.'

For a minute, Gerry stared at the paper, having difficulty in deciphering the scribble. Then, as she realized what she was reading, she gave a whoop of pure joy!

'A set of knock-on wire wheels? Oh, Jeremy! The whole set – in good condition, right?' She could hardly believe her eyes. She ran over and was about to throw her arms round him when she stopped. At the very bottom of the sheet of paper, her eyes had suddenly made out the price.

'But that's a fortune!' she exclaimed.

'They're pretty rare.' Jeremy took the paper from her fingers. 'Still, I agree. I think this is a bit steep. Look, leave it with me. I'll see if I can get them to pull the price down a bit.'

Gerry let out a deep sigh, then turned to grin sheepishly at her father. 'Wouldn't like me to stand in on the pumps at weekends, would you, Pa?' she offered.

She already knew what her father's reply would be.

'Forget it! I know,' she said for him. 'Mum would go spare because of my school work. And you'd have trouble with your labour force – not to mention the tax man, right? It was just a thought . . .' she finished. She cast a quick smile at her big brother. 'See if they'd be interested in part payment, will you?' she said. 'You know, like a little part now, and the rest in twenty years?'

Her father and brother laughed, and she did, too. Only it sounded rather hollow – and really, what she wanted to do was kick something! It was so frustrating: no matter how much enthusiasm she had, it always seemed to come down to money! But that was the trouble with having a hobby building 'real' cars instead of Lego kits, like most other people, she concluded miserably.

She walked down the stairs, back to the house, lost in dreams of raising the cash to be able to buy the four vintage wheels . . .

Life was funny, she decided as she opened the front door to hear the telephone ringing – it seemed that for every 'up' you got, there soon followed a 'down'! Take last Sunday, for example – her date with Clive had been a definite 'up'. Now, five days later, knowing the MG's wheels were so near and yet financially so far was a very definite 'down'.

Absent-mindedly, she picked up the phone as she passed the extension in the hall, then collapsed on a hall chair.

It was Clive!

Chapter 9

It had been one of the silliest conversations she'd ever had, Gerry decided after putting down the phone half an hour later. Silly, and funny – and great!

It had started off with Clive saying he was sorry he hadn't telephoned her. 'I've been sick,' he said.

'I know – Monte told me,' she replied.

'What!' he almost shouted. 'Has he asked you out?'

She giggled at that. He sounded jealous – actually jealous! 'Of course he hasn't! He's dating Patsie,' she told him.

'And some . . .' Clive said. Then stopped, adding, 'Don't quote me on that score, okay?'

'Okay,' she agreed, but not too happily. After all, Patsie was keener on Monte than she'd been on any of her other boyfriends.

'I've got a bad case of the spots,' Clive informed her.

'Lucky you!' she threw back.

'I'm looking for sympathy,' he said, sounding peeved – but laughing.

'I'm looking for several hundred quid for four wheels,' she replied, ignoring the hurt tone of his voice.

'What's more important? Me – or your wheels? Where's your heart?'

'Okay, I'm sorry about the spots, but they'll go. My wheels are likely to disappear too, but whereas you'll get better, I'll be worse off.'

He really laughed then. 'I'm getting the impression that any boyfriend of yours has to play second fiddle to your dream car, right?'

'But I haven't got a boyfriend,' she said. She hadn't meant to say it, it just slipped out.

'So what about me?' he asked, banteringly. 'I've already signed up for violin lessons, not to mention an advanced course in mechanics!'

'Clive, you're crazy!' she informed him, beginning to feel all sort of marsh-mallowy inside.

'Only about you!' he replied.

She felt her throat go dry and her voice, when she finally found it, came out all squeaky.

'Me?'

'You!' he continued. 'And, of course, about that car you're making. I reckon you'll make quite a pair.'

'Be serious!' She was growing amazingly brave, feeling safe with the telephone between them. Face to face, she'd probably have been so shy she wouldn't have been able to think, let alone speak!

'But I am serious,' he replied. 'Look, I won't be out of quarantine for at least another week, maybe two. But promise me you won't go out with anyone – not even heart-throb Pole – until I see you again.'

'I couldn't anyway,' she told him, kidding him along, 'I've got my Mocks – and that means even the MG stays under cover until they're over.'

'In that case, I'll relax and stop worrying myself into a nervous breakdown –' He stopped, then whispered down the line. 'I must go. The doctor's just arrived and I'm not supposed to be out of bed. 'Bye!'

'Who was that, pet?' her mother asked as she joined her in the kitchen.

Gerry smiled. 'Clive. He's sick – chicken pox.'

'Nasty!' her mother remarked, casting a glance over her shoulder as she peeled potatoes at the sink. 'I hope you're not going to catch it – heaven forbid!'

'Why should I? I'm fine. In fact,' she added breezily, walking on air to help her mother with the spuds, 'I feel wonderful!'

'That's the trouble. Everyone's fine until they go down with something. That's all we'd need, chicken-pox in the house!'

'Mother, where's your sympathy? Anyway, it needn't be me who brings it home. Apparently it's rife at the college – so it could be one of the boys brings it in.'

'Great!' her mother replied, plonking an enormous potato into Gerry's outstretched hand. 'Thanks for the heartening news!' She was about to go back to her half-peeled potato when something in Gerry's face caught her attention.

'What's suddenly so fantastic that you've got such a smile on your face, little girl?' she inquired, a hint of suspicion in her pale grey eyes. 'Don't tell me it's a boy – Clive, perhaps?'

Gerry felt light-headed and silly. 'Oh Mum, isn't he just smashing? I think I'm in love!' she replied expansively, throwing her arms wide and accidentally dropping her potato on the floor.

Her mother picked it up and said seriously, 'Gerry, pet, don't you think this might be a bit sudden?'

'Okay – if you won't buy that, how about Jeremy's found a garage that's got a set of knock-on wheels for me?'

'Now, that's more like it,' her mother said. 'How much?'

The smile wavered, then faded from Gerry's flushed face. Her voice fell. 'Too much.'

Her mother raised her brows. 'Really?'

''Fraid so. Jeremy's going to see if they'll bring down the price a bit.' She took the potato from her mother, then slowly began peeling it, lost in thought.

'Don't look so depressed, pet,' said her mother, seeing her changed expression. 'There's always your birthday, isn't there? It's not far away.'

For a second, Gerry's hopes soared – until she remembered she'd already earmarked the family for a respray for the car for her birthday present. And with any luck, her own socket set, too. And besides, she reckoned, to buy the whole set of wheels was pushing even her parents' generosity a bit too far.

Now, she shook her head. 'Forget it, Mum,' she said. 'I'll just have to think of a way to boost my savings, that's all. Maybe a part-time job –'

'Not until after you've finished your exams, Gerry!' Her mother's face was set. 'Maybe in the summer you could help out as holiday relief on the cash desk ... we'll see.'

The point was, would her wheels still be around by the summer hols? Gerry doubted it, and she might have wallowed in self-pity if another subject hadn't somehow bubbled up to the surface of her thoughts.

Clive Rowlings. She had a strange tingling suspicion that her mother could be wrong. She wasn't too sure about how it felt to be in love ... well, beginning to fall in love. But she had a feeling that the warm, melting feeling she experienced every time she thought of Clive was more than just infatuation.

Clive Rowlings ... she tried to picture him as she lay in bed that night, staring with unseeing eyes at her bedroom ceiling, bathed in moonlight.

She wondered if he was thinking of her, as he lay in his sick bed. She tried to imagine him covered in spots – and ended up giggling into her pillow. It was silly for an eighteen-year-old boy to get something as childish as chickenpox!

She turned over and snuggled down under her duvet, pulling it up to her chin. She hoped he liked her 'get well' card. She suppressed a yawn and tried to go to sleep.

I wish I'd signed it just Gerry, she suddenly thought. Or even put With Love ...

She wished a lot of other things, too, before sleep finally stole through the window with the moonbeams and lulled her into unconsciousness.

She dreamed of Clive and herself in her spanking new, deep-green racing car. It was vague exactly where they were heading but in her dreams, it didn't really matter. All that mattered was that they were together...

In the morning, the memory of the dream lingered on, making her smile as she stretched awake. She was ready to jump in her car right at that moment and make it come true – only that was out of the question, wasn't it?

The following week saw Gerry buckling down to some serious revision, ready for the Mocks. She wasn't particularly worried about any of her subjects, apart from Technical Drawing. There were only two girls taking TD – Gerry and Sandy, whose father was an architect. Gerry enjoyed the subject but found she spent a lot of time getting her work done, whereas Sandy seemed to find it very easy.

'Take my father's advice,' Sandy said when Gerry talked it over with her one lunchtime over a rather sad-looking toad-in-the-hole, 'don't be too much of a perfectionist. He said you can work up to perfection only with time, and that examiners don't expect us to be real experts.'

'He said that?'

Sandy nodded, observing Gerry through her spectacles. 'Well, I must say I spend a lot of time rubbing things out. Maybe I should finish the drawings first, then go back, if I've got time, to perfect my work.' She pushed the half-full plate of food away from her. 'Thanks for the tip,' she told her friend.

'Hi, Gerry!' Patsie called from the counter, where she'd just taken some fruit for her dessert. 'Want an apple?'

Gerry nodded, then watched Patsie walk over to join them. She was looking particularly pretty with her hair loose about her shoulders and, Gerry noticed, she was breaking school rules by wearing lip gloss and mascara – a sure sign that Monte was picking her up again after school. She wondered, not for the first time, how Patsie ever got any revision done. She seemed to be going out every night.

Now, as her friend sidled into the seat on the bench beside her, she said, 'Hi, Patsie. You look great today. Doesn't your mother mind you going out so much? Mum would be furious.'

Patsie bit into her red apple with perfect pearly teeth, and shrugged her shoulders indifferently.

'She's hardly ever in herself these nights, anyway. If she's not working at the hospital, she's dating some dishy young doctor she's met.' She chewed thoughtfully for a second, then swallowed and looked pointedly at Gerry. 'Anyway, I tell her I'm meeting some of you, to study.'

'I've told you, Patsie, please don't include me in that again,' Gerry put in quickly. 'You've no idea how embarrassing it was when you did it last time – and I rang you up.'

Patsie tossed her head and laughed. 'You make such a thing about a little white lie. Honestly, Gerry, you're too good to be true!'

Gerry bit her lip. She wanted to say she didn't see the difference between little white lies and great big black ones. But she didn't.

'Anyway, don't worry, I'll leave you out of it.' Patsie's dark eyes narrowed as she turned back to her friend. 'Say – what news of El Spotto?' she asked.

Gerry's cheeks blazed. 'If you mean Clive, he's getting on fine. He called the other night – ' she stopped, not wanting to share what up till then had been personal. But it was too late.

'What? And you never told me? You're getting really sneaky lately,' Patsie said, pouting.

'It's Gerry's private life,' Sandy put in. 'She doesn't have to tell you, or any of us about it.'

Patsie pulled a long face at her, then turned back to Gerry. 'Are you going to see him? Is he out of quarantine yet?' Her tone had changed, and she sounded sincerely interested.

'Yes,' Gerry said, 'he's much better – so he said. His last spot has all but gone so the doc said it'd be okay for him to see friends now. He asked me round on Saturday afternoon.' She bit into her apple, feeling all warm and happy again. It was odd, just thinking of Clive now had that effect on her. As if she were sharing something special – a birthday treat every time! 'How are things with Monte – still going strong?' she asked, swinging the spotlight off her.

'Yeah, great!' Patsie said, although for a second, Gerry was certain there was a strained look in her friend's eyes.

'Really?' she prompted, studying her face.

Patsie took the last bite of her apple, then threw the core on the plate before her. 'He's mad about me!' She swung her long legs over the bench and stood up. 'Anyone coming for a walk over the playing fields?' she asked.

'I'll come.' Sandy stood up.

'Me, too,' Miranda echoed, finishing her yogurt.

'What about you, Gerry?' Patsie asked, pointedly.

Gerry shook her head. 'Count me out,' she said, then smiled wearily. 'I must do some more revision on my TD – the exam's in the morning.'

'Good luck!' Patsie said, then grinned and walked away, the two other girls running to catch up with her – leaving Gerry alone and wondering just for an instant, whether Patsie's last remark was said nicely or if she was being snide?

On Saturday it was raining. Not just a thin, fine drizzle, but really pelting down. Gerry stared through the misted window of her bedroom and wondered for the umpteenth time what she should wear to visit Clive that afternoon.

'Telephone, Gerry!' Sam stuck his head round her bedroom door. For a second, her stomach seemed to somersault inside her. 'Don't get panicky – it's not clever Clive,' her brother told her. 'It's some guy called – Monte? Sounds foreign to me . . .'

'Monte? But what does he want?' Gerry walked to the door, puzzled. Maybe something was wrong with Patsie . . .?

'I'd like to tell you, but I'm not proficient at clairvoyance yet,' Sam joked. Then he added, 'Don't be all day, though, I'm waiting for a call from a mate – about a double date this evening.'

Gerry giggled. 'What? You dating? Don't say you've discovered girls?'

'Well,' Sam followed her down to the hall, 'since you've found out there are boys as well as cars, I thought I'd better broaden my horizons, too.' He gave her a playful punch on the shoulder as she picked up the phone.

'Hi, Gerry! Great to hear your voice,' Monte said when she said hello. 'Look, I was wondering, if you're free tonight, how about taking in a film and a pizza?'

'Oh, well, I – er – I'm sorry,' she said, feeling something like panic, 'but I can't. I mean, I've got some revision to get through and besides, I appreciate you and Patsie thinking about me but – '

'What's Patsie got to do with this?' He laughed. 'This is me asking you for a date. I never did go in for crowds.'

For a second Gerry didn't know what to say, then she began to get angry. 'But you're going out with Patsie,' she said.

'Sure I go out with Patsie, but I'm not asking her to marry me, am I? I'm free to ask out other girls – girls I really feel attracted to. Like you. Say,' he paused long enough to draw breath, then asked, 'you're not engaged to old Clive, are you?'

She gave a short laugh. 'No, but that doesn't mean I'm agreeing to go out with you, Monte. Thanks. But sorry—'

'Just a sec!' he cut in. 'What has Clive got that I haven't, anyway?' He sounded really annoyed.

Gerry drew in her breath. 'I don't know,' she said, coldly, 'but when I find out, I'll let you know. 'Bye!' She hung up, furious.

When her anger subsided, she suddenly thought of Patsie. Somehow, she doubted that Patsie would be aware of the fact that her steady wasn't so steady after all. And she knew Patsie wouldn't take kindly to being told Monte was two-timing – no way! Gerry thought it was strange how even she had been fooled by Monte's charm that first time she and Patsie had met him. But poor Patsie – she was still fooled!

Gerry rang the Rowlings' doorbell just on four. She had dressed carefully in her tartan skirt and green blouse, with her raincoat on top. The door was opened almost instantly by Mrs Rowlings, who by the look of her mac and umbrella, and the shopping basket on her arm, was just on the way out.

'Hello, Gerry. Come to visit the invalid? Go on up, I'm just on my way to the bakery – I forgot the bread.' She stepped aside to let Gerry in. 'Trust me!' she said, smiling warmly. 'Fancy forgetting the bread. Normally, I'd ask Peter to go,' she explained, referring to her husband, 'but he's taken himself off to play snooker.'

'Would you like me to go for you?' Gerry offered. But Mrs Rowlings patted her arm and shook her head.

'No, no, you go and see Clive. Actually, you're the second visitor he's got this afternoon. Quite a celebrity he's turning out to be. Now, up you go.'

Gerry stepped into the warmth of the hall, and heard the door close behind her. For a moment she wondered if she should call out, then, hearing voices, decided not to. Who could the second visitor be, she mused, as she slipped off her coat and hung it on the hall stand? Then she made her way upstairs, following the buzz of voices to Clive's room.

Just as she reached the door, the voices died. With her fingertips pushing the door open, Gerry called out Clive's name.

It all happened in a blurred second – the door swinging silently ajar... the picture of Clive in striped pyjamas in bed... and Patsie, her long black hair swinging down her back, sitting next to him, her arms round his neck – kissing.

'Excuse me!' The words tumbled out before she could check them, pulling the two culprits apart. Gerry got a quick glimpse of Clive's confused, anxious face and Patsie's frozen smile.

Then she turned and ran downstairs. She grabbed her coat and opened the door – just as Clive appeared at the top of the landing.

'Gerry! Come back!' he called. 'It's not –'

Gerry slammed the front door and ran blindly along the deserted, grey-paved street, her tears blending with the rain.

Chapter 10

For the rest of Saturday and most of Sunday Gerry split her time between the Tin Barn and her room. It was amazing how much she could achieve by really applying herself to whatever job she had in hand. She attacked the rust on the running boards with the sand-blasting machine until her arms and back ached, and her hands were cramped and sore.

Then she'd take herself off to her room and immerse herself in her school work, blotting out everything else. That way she didn't have to think about Clive – or

Patsie – or the fact that somewhere deep inside, she hurt.

'You okay, pet?' her mother asked as she ate Sunday lunch with the rest of the family. 'You're very quiet.'

'She's in love!' Bobby said.

'That's enough, lad,' her father warned, casting a quick glance at Gerry's pale, set face.

'How was clever Clive?' Sam peered under her tousled curls as she sat, head drooped, over her half-eaten roast pork and vegetables.

'Fine!' Gerry forced herself to smile brightly. But she wasn't fooling anyone, it seemed.

'Leave her alone,' her mother said, clearing Gerry's plate from the table. 'She's got a lot on her mind at the moment, what with her exams coming up.'

Silently, Gerry blessed her for furnishing an excuse for her mood. But in the kitchen, later, her mother was more direct.

'Look, Gerry dear, I don't know what's happened in your life to affect you so, but I can guess. Let me just say, for all the right reasons, that your first love – well, it's hardly ever your last. So don't let whatever's upset you hang around for too long, eh?'

She wanted to run and hug her mother, to tell her how angry and betrayed she felt. Not only by Clive and her best friend, but by her own feelings, too.

Instead, she managed a tight, bright smile. 'I'm okay,' she said. Then, as her mother's questioning gaze lingered, she added, less brightly, 'Honestly.'

She busied herself furiously piling the dirty plates into the dishwasher, hoping against hope that no one would call her or ask her a question because she knew, given half the chance, she'd burst into fresh floods of tears.

No one was more surprised than Gerry when Patsie appeared at her bedroom door later that evening. She'd been so immersed in her Metalwork revision that she hadn't even heard the doorbell ring downstairs.

'Can I come in?' Patsie sidled into the room, her usually pretty, happy face pale and serious.

Gerry nodded, silently wondering what was coming. After all, it was clear Patsie had already got back what Gerry had once thought was hers – Clive's affection.

'I just want to tell you, you got it all wrong yesterday afternoon,' her friend said, awkwardly. 'I know what it must have *looked* like – but it wasn't.'

Gerry didn't help out. She just stared at Patsie, who stood hesitantly in the centre of the pale-blue carpet.

'You see,' Patsie went on nervously, twisting the strap of her handbag, 'I was supposed to meet Monte at Clive's. It was his suggestion, only he didn't turn up. And then he rang me – would you believe, at Clive's home? – to tell me he couldn't make it after all. In fact, I got the message loud and clear that I wouldn't be seeing him again.' Patsie's bottom lip began to tremble, then bright, crystal tears sprang into her eyes. Bravely, she tried to blink them aside. 'I was upset, as you may imagine – after all, I thought I was . . . well, special . . .' She made a small, hopeless gesture with her hands. 'After the call, Clive tried to tell me how it was with Monte. He said that when he brought Monte along that first night, he hadn't known him very well. It's just since then he's learned what Monte's really like. He told me that I was better off without him. That he wasn't the type of guy to get serious about. In fact, the home truths I've never wanted to face. But he was right, and I knew it. And that hurt even more.' She stopped, took a tissue from her bag, and blew her nose loudly. Her whole body was shaking.

Gerry couldn't stand seeing her best friend so upset. She jumped up from where she'd been at her desk and ran across to put an arm round Patsie's trembling shoulders. Then she led her across to the divan.

'I was kissing Clive's cheek to thank him for being so supportive when you walked in. Honestly, that was all there was to it,' Patsie said, sitting opposite Gerry.

The two friends gazed at each other for a moment.

'It's okay, I understand,' Gerry said, at last. 'I believe you.'

Between Patsie's tears, a small smile emerged. Gerry smiled back.

'If you'd seen your face!' Patsie said, dabbing her nose with her damp tissue. The smile widened.

'I bet!' Then Gerry started to giggle as she remembered the look on Patsie's face, too. 'Yours was quite a picture, come to think of it,' she told her friend. 'And Clive! Oh, poor Clive!' She was serious for a moment. 'Do you think I should ring him?'

Patsie tossed her hair off her wet cheeks. 'I think you should. Poor bloke. He was only trying to be a knight in shining armour – and he got treated like the big bad villain!'

'I guess you've got a point. I'll ring him.' Gerry sat staring at her hands for a few seconds, a thought forming in her mind.

At last she looked up at Patsie. 'Did you tell Monte you knew I was going to visit Clive yesterday afternoon?' she asked.

Patsie nodded, puzzled. 'Well, yes – why?'

'And did he suggest you met up at Clive's before, or after he knew I'd be there?'

The frown of confusion deepened on Patsie's smooth brow. 'Er . . . after,' she told Gerry. 'Why?'

Gerry stood up and walked over to the window. She gazed outside at the neat garden and across to the garage. 'I'm glad you've finished with him,' she finally announced. 'Because I don't think he's very nice at all.' She turned to face Patsie, wondering for a moment if she should confess that Monte had wanted to date her. Then she dropped the idea. Why should she add to her friend's misery? It was obvious now that Monte had deliberately set up yesterday's misunderstanding. At least, it all pointed that way. He'd arranged it so that Patsie would be at Clive's alone – and that's how Gerry would find them. He also must have known that his farewell phone call would upset Patsie, and that she would probably confide in Clive. He may not have reckoned on the actual scene that ensued, but in Gerry's mind his aim was clear – he wanted to cause trouble between the three of them. Or, at least, between her and Clive.

'What is it, Gerry?' Patsie was eyeing her suspiciously. 'What are you thinking?'

She shrugged off the question. 'Forget it,' she said. Then she asked, 'You're not too heartbroken, are you?'

'Yes, but I suppose it'll mend,' came her friend's reply. 'The trouble is,' a sigh escaped Patsie's pale lips, 'what on earth am I going to do every evening – let alone at weekends?'

'Weekdays you work!' Gerry told her sternly. 'After all, you've got a mass of catching up to do for your exams, right?'

Patsie pulled a wry face, agreeing. 'But what about weekends?' she wailed. 'It's okay for you, you've got Clive *and* three brothers. And a super mum and dad.'

Gerry walked back across the room and sat down on the bed again. 'Why not come and join us?' she suggested. 'You're always welcome, as long as you keep your hands off married Mike – right?'

'Meanie!' Patsie replied. Then she said lightly, 'What about Bobby, or Jeremy?' There was a shine back in her eyes now.

'Well, Bobby's got a steady – well, sort of. But Jeremy's game – and don't forget Sam. Hey – you could end up as my sister-in-law!' Gerry burst out laughing.

'Someone call my name?' Sam's copper head appeared round the bedroom door.

'Go away!' Gerry told him.

Sam ignored her and came further into the room, his dark-blue eyes, so like his sister's, directed on Patsie. Clearly he liked what he saw. 'Mum says will Patsie stay for supper?' he said.

Patsie looked from Sam, to Gerry. 'Well . . . I don't know . . .' she began, but Sam brushed her hesitation aside.

'I'll say yes – okay?' He winked at Patsie, then left the two girls alone.

Patsie glanced across at Gerry, and found her smiling.

'As I said – what about Sam?' said Gerry suggestively.

'Oh, Gerry! What would I do without you?' Patsie sighed deeply, then took a last dab at her damp eyes.

Gerry stood up, then pulled her friend to her feet. 'Don't talk so daft!' she said. 'It's what friendship's all about, isn't it?'

It was eight o'clock that evening when Gerry rang Clive's number. He answered it so quickly she felt he must have been sitting on the phone.

'Patsie came round,' she told him, a little breathlessly. 'I just want to say I'm sorry.'

'Me too,' Clive answered.

'You? Why?'

'I'm sorry you were upset. And sorry we didn't get to talk. And sorry you thought – well, you know.'

'Clive?'

'Yes?'

She wanted to tell him – oh, so many things – but all that came out was, 'Er, 'night.'

''Night, Gerry,' he replied, then added before hanging up, 'I'll ring you – okay?'

'Okay – great!' she exclaimed happily. Then she was left hanging on to the phone, wondering if she'd sounded too keen. Thinking maybe she'd made a fool of herself. Convinced that he probably thought her far too young and inexperienced and, well, silly!

She wandered into the kitchen and decided to make herself a cup of hot chocolate before going back upstairs for more revising. Her mind was full of mixed-up thoughts, mostly about Clive.

'Hi, kid!'

Gerry looked up, realizing she wasn't alone in the kitchen. 'I'm not a kid!' she informed Bobby, who stood watching her as he waited for the kettle to boil.

For a moment, brother and sister stared at each other across the kitchen. Then Bobby reached out an arm towards her. It was so spontaneous, going back to when she was just a toddler and Bobby her big, protective brother, that Gerry didn't hesitate. She ran round and snuggled up to his broad, comforting chest. His arm looped round her narrow shoulders, holding her tight against him.

'Life bringing my little sister a whole new set of problems?' he asked.

Gerry rested her head against his chest, and let out a sigh. 'I think playing with cars is much less complicated than people,' she replied.

Bobby gave a wry laugh. 'You can say that again, little sis,' he said. 'Mine turned out to be married!'

Chapter 11

'So, how's it going?' Clive shouted above the sound of the sand-blasting machine.

Gerry peered through her protective visor and opened her eyes wide at the sight of Clive leaning against the door. Her heart fluttered wildly as she reached across to switch off the machine at the power point. She was suddenly aware of how she must look in her oil-stained workman's overalls with her hair scruffed back under her cap. She slipped the visor up to rest on the top of her head and smiled, sheepishly.

'Sorry? I didn't hear you, Clive,' she said, placing the machine on the workbench before turning back to face him. Clive in a pair of faded blue jeans and a black PINK FLOYD sweatshirt. She wondered for a moment just how long he'd been watching her, and began to blush.

'I said, how's it going – the car?' He pushed himself away from the door and walked over to join her.

'Oh, it's coming on,' she told him, pulling a face to indicate that it was a long job.

'Looks pretty impressive to me.' He walked over to examine the bodywork and newly welded chassis, which was propped up on a supporting block at the back of the barn.

Gerry pushed an imaginary curl off her forehead and left black grease streaked across her brow. 'How come you're here?' she asked, pleasantly.

'Sam brought me back from college,' Clive explained. 'We're going to play squash. Actually, I wangled it so that I could come over to see you. Don't mind, do you?'

'Mind?' She was delighted! 'I was hoping to see you,' she told him. 'I wanted to apologize properly for acting like a nerd last week.' She squinted across at him, the sun in her eyes as it streamed through the barn door behind him.

'Gerry, you might be many things, but a nerd? Never!' He walked across to where she was standing by the running boards. 'You know, I never thought I'd ever see a girl look so fantastic in a fella's overalls.' His eyes ran over her from head to toe. 'Especially ones that are three sizes too big, and covered in grease,' he added.

He was grinning, but Gerry still felt awkward. Not from what he'd just told her but because there was a certain soft, tender look in his eyes as he scrutinized her upturned face.

'They're Jeremy's,' she spluttered, looking away from his direct gaze and grabbing a tin of sump oil which was resting on the bonnet – anything to steady the trembling of her hands.

'Gerry?' Her name on his lips was almost a whisper.

She looked up – but couldn't speak because her throat had dried up on her again and her tongue seemed to be stuck to the top of her mouth. Hesitantly, she raised her large blue eyes to meet his. The next second seemed to pass in slow motion. Clive moved close to her – so close she could feel his heart beating against hers. Then she was in his arms, and all other thoughts vanished as he lowered his lips to hers.

'You're really quite a girl,' he told her.

The kiss seemed to last for ever. When he drew away, she was breathless. 'I've wanted to do that for ages,' he told her.

'Oh!' Gerry exclaimed in a soft whisper. She drew in a deep breath to try to clear her head. 'Oh!' she exclaimed again, but this time it came out as a loud yelp.

Clive glanced down to where Gerry was staring, wide-eyed in horror. The sump oil was slowly running out of the tin, down his jeans, to form a large, black puddle all over his trainers! Gerry stared from the spilled oil to the can she was still holding in her hand, and back to Clive, horrified.

'That'll teach me to get involved with a mechanic, won't it?' he groaned. 'Boy! Having you for a girlfriend is never going to be dull – I can see that!'

'You're not mad?' Gerry asked in relief.

'Of course I'm mad,' he replied, pulling her into the circle of his arms. 'Mad to get tied up with a maniac like you!'

'But you're not,' she said, adding, 'tied up with me.'

'Is that what you think?' He didn't wait for her reply because her brother suddenly called him from the forecourt. 'I'd better go and change into my squash gear before I get into Sam's bad books.' He let her go and began to hurry towards the entrance to the barn. Then he stopped, and turned to face her again. 'I know you're going to be busy these next few weeks, what with your exams, but I wondered. Will you come with me to the Custom Car Rally at Knebworth? It's on Bank Holiday Monday.'

'Sounds great!' she replied, happily. 'Is that a date?'

Clive gave a mock salute. 'It's a date, lady!' Then, as he was about to leave, he called back. 'By the way, I wanted to tell you something.'

Gerry's eyes brightened in anticipation. 'Yes?'

He grinned. 'You've got grease smeared all over your face.'

Her fingers shot to her cheeks. 'Don't worry, though. It suits you!' he told her. Then he ducked as the empty oil can whizzed through the air towards him.

As the term advanced, Gerry settled down to do her best with her exams. When she wasn't studying, she relaxed with her car, doing as much as her limited funds would allow. Even so, the car was really coming together, especially as she'd managed to get Patsie interested in it, too. Though Gerry couldn't help feeling that the attraction in lending her a hand wasn't so much interest in building the car as a growing attraction for her brother Bobby. Much to Sam's pique!

She didn't see much of Clive, but she understood. As he'd explained during one of their regular, long telephone conversations, he had a mass of catching up to do because he'd been off sick and he had his end-of-the-college-year exams looming in June.

'That's okay – I know how you must feel,' Gerry told him. 'I'm up to my ears in work, too.'

'How's the MG coming along?' he asked her.

'Slowly – not just because of my studying but because I've got to the part where it's expensive. I must get a job in the summer to earn some money to buy the set of wheels Jeremy's tracked down for me.'

'Pricey, eh?'

Gerry let out a short laugh. 'A bit.'

'Look – don't forget what Uncle Ted said. If there's anything he can help with? He meant it.'

'I haven't forgotten,' she replied. Then she thought about the new starter motor she needed, and explained. 'The engine I've got's fine. Mike checked it over. But I'll need a new starter motor. So far I haven't seen one for sale anywhere. And I've advertised in the various car magazines, too.'

'Okay, I'll talk to Uncle Ted tonight. He may be able to come up with one – with luck. You never know.'

'It would be great. Thanks.' Gerry was about to put down the phone when Clive called her back. 'Yes?'

'You haven't forgotten about our date at Knebworth, have you?' he asked her.

'Don't worry, I won't let you off the hook that easily, Clive Rowlings – no way!'

Gerry smiled to herself as she walked up to her

bedroom. It was strange, she mused, how relaxed she was with Clive now, considering how it had been at the beginning. How nervous and awkward she'd felt just talking to him. 'It was the same when you had to talk to any boy – don't kid yourself!' she said out loud.

She walked past her wardrobe, then stopped and retraced her steps to look at her image in the mirror. Her eyes took in her new haircut, which gently framed her face in a soft, feminine style. Now, instead of standing out like an errant halo, her hair curled into the nape of her neck and fanned her high cheekbones. She turned sideways, aware of her trim figure silhouetted in her new pencil-slim skirt and neat, stack-heel shoes. The bat-winged, short-line jumper in the latest mulberry pink contrasted with her pale skin and accentuated the unusual depth of her eyes.

I've changed, she thought pensively, looking at herself. And she knew it had a lot to do with Clive . . . Clive and the fact that in July, just over a month, she'd be at that magical age – seventeen!

'It was peculiar,' Patsie said, looking up from applying a coat of Gerry's new orangy varnish to her nails, 'but once the exams actually started, all my nerves disappeared!'

Gerry nodded. 'I know what you mean. It's almost as if the worst part of having exams is the thought of having them, not actually sitting them. Very odd.'

The two friends were relaxing in Gerry's bedroom. Patsie was sitting at the desk, while Gerry was sprawled on her stomach on the carpet, sorting through a pile of albums Patsie had brought over.

'This looks good,' Gerry said, lifting out Arcadia's

latest recording. She studied Simon Le Bon's face for a while, then turned to show it to Patsie. 'Don't you think Clive looks a bit like him, only darker?' she asked, dreamily.

'What? No! Nothing at all! You need glasses if you think so. Simon Le Bon's good-looking!'

Gerry stuck her tongue out at Patsie's grinning face. 'Jealous! That's what you are.'

'Oh, come off it!' Patsie held her hands away from her at arm's length to admire the effect of the ten newly painted nails. 'Now, take your brother Bobby . . .'

'You're kidding! I mean, Bobby's great – but hardly good-looking.'

'You don't see him through my eyes.' Patsie smiled mischievously, hugging her knees to her chin, her bare feet resting on the edge of the seat.

'That's true!' Gerry stood up, then stretched. She was happy – not just because it was Friday and the exams were over, but because tomorrow Clive was taking a break from his studying to come round and spend the afternoon with her.

When she'd told her mother, she'd suggested he stay for supper.

'We could have a spaghetti party, if you like,' she said. 'You know how the boys love it.'

'That'd be great,' Gerry enthused.

'And ask Patsie,' her mother said. 'I'm sure she'd love to come, too.'

'Okay.' Gerry was glad her mother had included Patsie. Recently, her friend had seemed really down, and although Patsie didn't say much, Gerry had a feeling it had a lot to do with her mother who was seeing a lot of her doctor friend – which meant that

Patsie wasn't seeing a lot of her. When Gerry had tried to get her friend to talk about it, she'd shrugged it off, saying it didn't matter. But Gerry realized that wasn't true. It did matter a lot to Patsie.

'I bet you get a bit fed up with always having a crowd round you when you see Clive, don't you?' Patsie now asked.

The question took Gerry off-guard. 'Well . . .' she began, then made a small helpless gesture. 'A bit. But Mum's not too keen on me getting serious – she says I'm too young.'

'And what do *you* think?'

Gerry's cheeks grew hot. 'No comment!' she replied. But secretly, she was really looking forward to her date with Clive at the Custom Car Rally at Knebworth. They'd have a whole day together – just the two of them.

Gerry never quite worked out how Knebworth came up the next day as the whole family, including Clive and Patsie, sat round the dining-table tucking into her mother's spaghetti special.

'The Rally at Knebworth is coming up in a few weeks,' Sam said. 'Anyone interested in going?'

Jeremy nodded, his mouth full of spaghetti. 'I've been thinking about it. I hear it should be pretty good.'

'How about you Clive?' Sam asked. 'You're into custom cars, aren't you?'

Clive glanced at Gerry, who gave him a quick smile. 'Um, yeah, I am,' he answered hesitantly. 'As a matter of fact, Gerry and I already have plans to go to the rally.'

Bobby nervously cleared his throat and looked

across the table at Patsie. 'Are you interested in custom cars, Patsie?'

'Well . . . ' she began, but when Bobby interrupted.

'I mean, would you like to go to the rally with me?' he asked all in a rush.

Patsie's eyes lit up with delight. 'Sure!' she replied, and everyone around the table grinned, except Sam who looked on in envy.

'Isn't the rally on Bank Holiday Monday?' Gerry's father piped up. 'The garage will be closed, so we can all go to Knebworth together and make a day of it.'

Gerry's mother immediately picked it up as a super idea. 'I'll plan a picnic for us all – cold cuts and potato salad . . . some pies, I think. And fruit – oh, it'll be wonderful!' She grabbed Gerry's arm, giving it a squeeze. 'Don't you think it's a great idea, pet?'

Gerry managed a weak smile, then turned pleadingly to Clive, who gave her a quick, conciliatory look, and shrugged his shoulders.

So much for their day out alone together! Gerry pushed her fork into her mound of spaghetti and absently-mindedly twiddled it round and round, wondering if she and Clive would ever have a date together – on their own. By the time she lifted her fork to her mouth, the mound of spaghetti was the size of a golf ball!

'Gerry? Whatever are you doing?' Her mother stared at her.

'What?' Gerry glanced down at the enormous forkful of straggling pasta. She dropped it back on to her plate, then groaned out loud as it fell off and liberally splattered the spotless white cloth with blotches of tomato sauce.

'Somehow, I don't think you're with us, girl,' her father observed, with a twinkle in his eye. 'We haven't upset any special plans you and Clive had for the rally, have we?'

Gerry felt everyone's eyes on her. 'Of course not!' she bluffed. 'I'd better get a cloth to clean this mess,' she said, rising from the table. But in her hurry, her hand caught her glass of coke. She couldn't believe her eyes as, seconds later, the brown fizz joined the tomato sauce!

In desperation, Gerry cast a quick glance at Clive. What must he think of her? Then her embarrassment vanished. He was gazing at her with a special, loving look in his eyes.

Chapter 12

Gerry didn't even care that it rained most of the day — they had such a fantastic time. And even though there had been ten of them altogether, including the two grandmothers, Gerry spent most of the day very close to Clive.

They'd driven up to Knebworth House, near Letchworth in Hertfordshire, in three cars in the end: her mother, father and the two grans in the family car; her brothers and Patsie in Jeremy's — leaving Gerry to go alone with Clive in his father's. Once they were on the motorway, at the end of the convoy, Clive turned on the stereo and they relaxed, happy in each other's company.

'You know, it's odd, but I feel we've known each other all our lives,' Clive observed, glancing warmly across to her.

Gerry nodded. 'I know what you mean,' she said. 'I read once, somewhere, that if you feel like that with someone it's because you've met in another life. That you're sort of soul mates.' She chewed on her bottom lip, thinking, her chin resting in her hand. 'What do you think?' Her large deep-blue eyes took in Clive's perfect profile.

'Could be. I don't know,' Clive replied. 'But whatever the reason, it's nice.' He glanced at her. '*Very* nice,' he added.

They parked the cars under the trees in the area allotted for the spectators, then decided to split up into their various groups.

'We'll meet back here in an hour,' Mrs Jones told everyone. 'That will give us time for our picnic before the events begin.' She glanced at the two older women, who were standing either side of her. 'I think we'll go and take a tour round Knebworth House – it will be easier than walking round in this drizzle.' The two grandmas agreed.

'I'm going to go visit the kids' amusement park,' Sam announced. 'Anyone coming?'

Bobby and Patsie decided to go with Sam, which left Jeremy and Gerry's father – apart from Gerry and Clive.

'Well, I came here to see the rally, so I'm going to make my way down to the track – coming, Jeremy?' Mr Jones turned to leave. Then he added, to Gerry, 'If you two feel like joining us, we'll see you down there.'

'Fine, Mr Jones,' Clive replied. 'I'm just going over to see the listing of events at the main centre. We'll come down after that – I'll get us some programmes, too.'

'Good thinking, lad,' Mr Jones replied, waiting for Jeremy to catch up with him before they began tramping through the grass, heading to the bottom field where the circuit was marked out.

Now they were alone together Clive slipped an arm round Gerry's waist. And even though they were wearing raincoats, she could feel the pressure of his fingers – the warmth of his body close to hers.

'Come on,' he said, walking her under the trees towards the distant group of low-lying buildings. But Gerry stopped beneath a huge old oak which acted as a screen between them and the rest of the family.

'Something wrong?' he asked, looking down at her rain-splashed face.

'Kiss me,' she told him, simply.

'What?' He seemed genuinely surprised.

'Kiss me,' she repeated, and held up her pointed chin so that her face was tilted to his.

'Well, if that's what you want –'

'Stop talking and do it!' She pouted her lips and closed her eyes, like a small girl waiting for a present.

Clive gathered her into his arms and gently covered her lips with his own. At first tenderly, then, as Gerry wound her arms round his neck, his kiss became harder, more demanding.

Gerry felt a warm pleasure spreading through her. She was aware of a raindrop trickling down her forehead to splash past her closed eyes. She smelt the tangy aftershave on Clive's cheeks, and thought she had to be near heaven!

All too soon, Clive released his clasp and smiled down at her with a puzzled expression.

'Well – what was all that about?' he asked.

Gerry stood swaying gently, then linked both arms round one of his and hung on tight. 'I didn't want to leave here without kissing you, silly. And this could be the only time we're alone together – okay?'

He ran his fingers through her damp curls and hugged her to him. 'Okay!' he agreed. 'Now come on, or we'll miss everything – including your folks, the food and the racing!'

Gerry had a brilliant time at the rally. She marvelled at some of the more amazing custom cars, and cheered them on during the races. One of her favourite events was the 'Run What Ya Brung' event. She'd never seen such a strange collection of cars at one time. They were all shapes and sizes and some of them were painted with incredible airbrushing – while others seemed to have parts missing! And the way the drivers threw them round the track was incredible. Hair-raising! But what impressed Gerry even more were the drag-racing cars. She had never seen anything like them before – outside of a sci-fi film! Some of the cars, she decided, were sheer fantasy and how they ever ran had to be the eighth wonder of the world!

'They're much too pretty to race!' she said to Clive as she stood in the rain watching the brightly coloured cars complete the circuit. She thought they looked like a bunch of exotic butterflies circling an old tyre, their brilliance enhanced even more against the dirt track.

'It's not so much a race,' Clive explained, 'as a sort of

public display. Notice, they're very careful not to get too near each other.'

It was true. But Gerry didn't blame any of the drivers. If she'd spent that much time on getting a car together, she'd feel the same. Why, she was even getting worried about the day the MG would be roadworthy!

As if reading her thoughts, Clive said, 'You could always keep your MG just for rallies. There's one in November at Bingley Hall – their Classic Restoration Show. You should think about getting the car ready for it.'

Gerry gave a wistful smile. 'I've a long way to go yet,' she said.

But she didn't realize just how far until they all arrived back home.

At first, when she saw the fire engines, Gerry was afraid that the house had caught fire. A crowd was being held back by police in the forecourt. In the gathering dusk, lights flashed and flickered and thick acrid smoke filled the air, together with soot and bits of grit. The smell of burning rubber and wood was everywhere.

Gerry hung on to Clive's hand as they ran after her parents towards the scene of the fire. They pushed past the mass of spectators and Gerry saw through the swirling smoke that it wasn't the house or the garage that had caught fire – it was the Tin Barn.

Miraculously, nothing else had caught, the police officer told her father as they stood watching the firemen wheel in their hoses through the puddles around them.

'It looks worse than it is, Mr Jones,' the Inspector said, later, jotting down some notes. They'd all gathered solemnly round the table. 'It could have been a disaster – what with the garage being so close.'

'Exactly!' Mr Jones conceded.

'It appears to have been caused by a short-circuit – but the insurance assessors will be here in the morning and no doubt they'll make a more thorough investigation. Well,' he closed his notepad with a snap, 'you'll be wanting to sort yourselves out, I dare say, so I'll leave you. And don't worry, it's perfectly safe now. The Chief Fireman's made a special inspection himself, and given the all-clear.'

Gerry's father saw the officer to the front door.

'Nothing too valuable in that barn, I trust?' the policeman asked.

'No,' Gerry heard her father reply. 'Nothing – except a car my daughter was building.' His voice seemed to crack. 'And that was priceless, I'm afraid.'

Gerry recognized the sadness in his voice, and at the same time felt the tightness in her throat as the tears began to well up in her eyes. With a supreme effort, she swallowed them away. By the time her father walked slowly back to the table she was smiling brightly.

'Don't go worrying about that old wreck,' she told him. 'I doubt if it would ever have got finished, anyway. As a mechanic, I'm a bit of a failure.' She'd meant it to come out all bright and bubbly – but from the look on everyone's face, she'd fooled no one.

'If it's any consolation,' her father said, slumping on to a chair and resting his head in his hands, 'we'll be able to claim on the insurance. But that doesn't help all that much, girl, does it? It doesn't pay for all the hard work and effort you've put in.'

Gerry left Clive's side, and walked over to stand beside her father. She placed her hands on his shoulders, then bent to kiss his lined cheeks.

'Dad, it doesn't matter, honestly,' she told him. 'All that matters is that nothing else was burned, and we're all safe. That's what's important.'

Her father reached up and covered her hands with his. 'You're a sweet kid,' he told her, 'and we'll make it up to you, you'll see.'

'I'll put the kettle on,' Gerry's mother said, her voice heavy with unshed tears.

It was too much for Gerry; she suddenly stood up and confronted them all. 'Look, will you all please stop acting as though this is a funeral!' she said. 'It was only an old pile of scrap metal – okay? I had fun with it and I learned a lot. In fact, it probably did me a favour – the fire. The next car I rebuild will be much better, because I'll have learned from the mistakes I made this time.' Again she smiled brightly and was relieved when her father stood up and hugged her to him.

'You know, everyone,' he said, holding Gerry even closer, 'I vote we all lend a hand in helping Gerry with her next project.'

There was a ripple of agreement, but Gerry shook her head.

'That's not the idea, Dad,' she said. 'After all, remember when you made your first car – didn't you say the greatest enjoyment was knowing you'd done it all on your own?'

'You've got a point, girl – but just to help you on your way, I think you should know that we all clubbed together and bought you that set of knock-on wheels. Only we were keeping them a secret until your birthday. And Mike was going to do your respray for you, as a gift. So, at least in a way, you'll be starting out ahead, so to speak.'

'And just for the record,' Clive added, 'I've got you a starter motor – that was for your birthday, too.'

Gerry felt the tears welling up again and swallowed hard. Only this time, they wouldn't go away.

'All I need now,' she said, 'is – ' she shrugged, then tried to smile through her tears – 'the rest of the car!'

She ran out of the room, with Clive close behind her. She didn't speak for a moment – it was taking all her effort just to come to terms with what had happened. They walked out into the garden, neither of them saying a word.

Gerry felt the cool, rain-washed air on her face and the breeze tugging at her hair. She stopped by the rose bed and smelt the first roses of summer, their heady fragrance mingling with the smell of smoke. Then she looked up and saw the stars, the mass of diamond-bright stars glittering across the deep blue of the moon-lit sky. Slowly, the dull pain began to disappear. She felt very small and insignificant beneath the vast heavens.

'You know,' she said at last, aware of Clive so close beside her, 'I always say that for every "up", there has to be a "down". And today, it was such a super "up" – I suppose, well, losing the car has to be the "down".'

She turned to face Clive and he was surprised to see that she wasn't crying any more. Her pretty face, with its huge, saucer eyes, was composed and a ghost of a smile even played round her lips.

'But really,' she went on, 'I've still got everything that really counts, haven't I? Everything I love. So what's a little "down"?'

Gerry could see he understood what she was talking about – that she'd still got her family and her home, in that all-embracing circle of love. She smiled at Clive, confirming that he too was inside her special circle. Then she sighed softly and reached up to link her hands behind Clive's neck.

'Kiss me?' she asked, remembering that other kiss – a whole lifetime away – under the old oak tree.

He kissed her gently and Gerry felt his love warm her heart. Then, with Clive's arms round her, she began to walk back across the damp, moonlit grass to the bright, welcoming lights of her home.

Tomorrow was another day . . .

Pam Lyons
Danny's Girl £1.25

For sixteen-year-old Wendy, life was pretty straightforward. She enjoyed her tomboy existence with her parents and brother Mike on their farm in Norfolk. Then, late one sunny September afternoon, Danny wandered into her life and suddenly Wendy's happy and uncomplicated world is turned upside-down. Unsure of how she should behave or what is expected of her, she allows herself to be carried along in Danny's wake, and when he finds himself in trouble at his exclusive boarding school she is his only ally. Eventually, Wendy's fierce loyalty to the boy she loves leads them both deeper and deeper into trouble . . .

Latchkey Girl £1.25

Ronnie was an only child and, compared with her young, glamorous parents with their interesting lives, pretty much of an 'ugly duckling' too. Only Gran, it seems, really loves her. But, when Gran's illness means she must come and live with her son and his family, Ronnie's problems come to a head and she is forced into a bold choice . . .

Ms Perfect £1.25

When Dawn's family enter her for the Ms Perfect competition, she is thrown into the whirl, swirl and glamour of a top national magazine. She is made up, dressed, interviewed and then photographed by a dishy photographer called Darren who wants Dawn to let him handle her modelling career. But at sixteen, Dawn isn't convinced that's what she wants. Besides, there's Ginger back home and, though he jokes about her looks and calls her Scruff, she can't imagine not having him around. And yet . . .

All these books are available at your local bookshop or newsagent, or can be ordered direct from the publisher. Indicate the number of copies required and fill in the form below.

Send to: **CS Department, Pan Books Ltd., P.O. Box 40, Basingstoke, Hants. RG21 2YT.**

or phone: 0256 469551 (Ansaphone), quoting title, author and Credit Card number.

Please enclose a remittance* to the value of the cover price plus: 60p for the first book plus 30p per copy for each additional book ordered to a maximum charge of £2.40 to cover postage and packing.

*Payment may be made in sterling by UK personal cheque, postal order, sterling draft or international money order, made payable to Pan Books Ltd.

Alternatively by Barclaycard/Access:

Card No. ☐☐☐☐☐☐☐☐☐☐☐☐☐☐☐☐☐☐☐☐

Signature:

Applicable only in the UK and Republic of Ireland.

While every effort is made to keep prices low, it is sometimes necessary to increase prices at short notice. Pan Books reserve the right to show on covers and charge new retail prices which may differ from those advertised in the text or elsewhere.

NAME AND ADDRESS IN BLOCK LETTERS PLEASE:

....

Name ─────────────────────────────

Address ────────────────────────────
─────────────────────────────────
─────────────────────────────────
─────────────────────────────────

3/87